I0818702

OTHER BOOKS BY LIZ RAIN

Onside Play
Perks of Office

Liz Rain

The MEET and GREET

ACKNOWLEDGMENTS

Thank you to Astrid Ohletz and Ylva Publishing for allowing me to live out my childhood dream of being a published author. It has been a real pleasure to take this book from concept to finished product with you.

Thanks to content editor Lenir Costa at Ylva for knowing when more melody needed to be added, and copy editor Michelle Aguilar for making the rhythm flow.

A very big thank you to Declan Smith, my wonderful sensitivity reader. As you so perfectly put it—if you've met one autistic person, you've met one autistic person.

This book is partly a love letter to all the pop divas I adore so much. I send my thanks and appreciation for you out into the universe.

I acknowledge the traditional owners of the land on which this book was written—the Turrbul and Jaggera peoples of the Yugambeh language region. I also acknowledge the traditional owners of the various lands where parts of this story are set. Aboriginal and Torres Strait Islander people are Australia's first storytellers, communicators, and creators of culture. I pay my respects to their elders, past and present.

DEDICATION

For Dani. You're my favourite singer, even though you forget all the words.

AUTHOR'S NOTE

This story features a character with autism spectrum disorder, and she shares past experiences of being misunderstood and talked down to. I've tried to get across that her autism is a part of who is she is, but not all she is.

She reflects one individual perspective and is not meant to be a stand-in for all autistic people.

CHAPTER 1

"Align steering wheel, check rear-view, right at a forty-five-degree angle, invert...and, done." Jane pressed the button to switch the car off.

"Whoa, one-shot reverse parallel park. Driving goals right there," Sara said as she jumped out. "And on the wrong side of the road too."

Jane joined Sara on the footpath and admired the lovely, even distance she had managed to get from the curb. "Like I said in your driving lessons—stick to your process, and you can manage any situation."

Sara flung her arm around her aunt's shoulders, and they headed towards Wilshire Boulevard. "You're the only Aussie I know who's not shit scared to drive in LA."

"I first learned to drive in Sydney. The drivers there are a lot more unpredictable than the polite Brisbane motorists you're used to. The freeways here still scare me, though."

Sara took a deep breath and flung her head back.

Jane inhaled the dry winter evening air as well. There was no escaping the high concentration of car exhaust pollution, but she didn't say anything. Sara would only call her a worry wart. Tonight was all about fun, after all. Jane needed it after the year she'd had.

They rounded a corner, and a queue of people came into view, snaking up towards the brightly lit El Rey Theatre.

Jane smiled as Sara skipped and clapped her hands. Sara had expressed joy through movement ever since she was a baby. At twenty years old, she showed no signs of stopping, so she probably never would.

As they joined the end of the queue, Jane assessed the other concertgoers. They were almost exclusively women in their late twenties or early thirties. Jane was nearing forty, so she and Sara fell outside the typical age range.

Jane cleared her throat and tapped her fingertips on the side of her leg. She often shied away from doing things that would cause the people around her to have big reactions, even if they were positive ones.

"Sara."

"Yes, Aunt Jane." She smirked, making fun of Jane's sudden formality of tone. She usually called her just Jane, or sometimes Jane-O.

Jane inclined her head then continued. "I know how much you enjoy this singer's music, so I upgraded our tickets to premium platinum, front-row balcony—oof!"

Sara had clamped her into a tight hug and was emitting an "eeeeeee" noise right next to her ear.

Jane smiled. "OK! Listen for a moment. The package also includes a private meet and greet after the concert."

"Ahhhhh!" Sara wrapped Jane up in another massive hug, bouncing her up and down but not quite able to lift her. "Oh my God! I don't fricken believe it! What the heck am I going to say to her? Eeeee! Thank you, thank you, thank you!"

Jane righted herself and straightened her button-down shirt. "You're very welcome." She cleared her throat again. "Plus, well, this outing was going to end up costing a little less than I originally planned for."

Sara's eyebrows creased. "Because you had to resell Lauren's ticket."

Jane nodded. "Luckily there are enough fans of this singer in LA that someone on the website wanted it."

"Hold on." Sara narrowed her eyes. "You have no idea who we're going to see tonight, do you?"

"Um, well—I know the name. It's..." Jane had her back to the theatre but jerked her head around, trying to read the illuminated black-and-white marquee.

Sara jumped in front of her, holding her backpack up to block the view.

Jane jumped. "It's—oof!" She landed awkwardly. Then, with a swift movement, she dodged around her niece and read the marquee.

"Amber Hatfield!" she said, still trying to catch her breath.

There was a smattering of applause from the group in front of them in line. "Got there in the end, love!" said a bloke in a puffer vest in a broad Australian accent.

Jane flushed and leaned towards Sara. "You know it's not that I don't care about you and your interests. Some things just don't stick in my head like they should: pop star things, reality TV things, and that TikTok dance you attempted to teach me. I'm sorry."

"Oh shit, no! Don't apologise!" Sara flung her arms around her. "I shouldn't have teased you. You wouldn't be you without your epic blind spot for all things pop culture. Plus, it's more important that things like baseline anthropological studies and peer-reviewed sociology theory papers stick in your head. Just let everything else slide right off, like, you know, a club sandwich off a car roof."

Jane chuckled. "To quote the famous old saying."

Sara gripped Jane's arm. "Oo! The line's moving."

They fell into step as the queue became a slow procession.

"I can't believe you didn't know about Amber Hatfield. She's the definition of a household name. An Aussie legend. It's like never having heard of Vegemite."

Jane glanced skywards for a moment. "I've heard of Vegemite. I guess your Jade Caulfield is a household name in every house but one."

Sara snorted with laughter. "You're low-key hilarious, you know that? Jade Caulfield." She chuckled and shook her head.

Jane's eyes darted back up to the marquee. "Ha ha, yes, got you. Just kidding. *Amber Hatfield* is the name of the musician we're about to see."

The queue stopped again, and they stood for a while, the twilight fading into night-time as Sara chatted to the other fans, scrolled on her phone, and read some of a thick paperback with a unicorn on the cover.

Excited murmurs from the front of the queue reached them, and Jane put away her copy of *Sociological Paradigms and Organisational Analysis* and trudged along with the line.

As they neared the doors, Jane tried to quash the trepidation that was buzzing around her insides. *Pop music isn't all that bad, even at an intense volume, for potentially hours at a time.* She let out a "tsk!". She had forgotten her earplugs. *I'll have sore feet and lifelong hearing loss from this show.*

Jane rolled back her shoulders and reminded herself that doing something different might be the best thing for her.

CHAPTER 2

Amber crashed down into the chair in front of her dressing room mirror. Her skin was hot and had a sheen of sweat. She closed her eyes and took three deep breaths.

Her assistant hovered behind her holding two towels. He stayed silent.

"Gorgeous energy tonight, Teddy," she finally said, opening her eyes and holding up her hand.

Teddy handed her the hot towel, and she started patting at her neck. The sweat had to come off, but there wasn't time before the meet and greet for a new face of make-up, or new hair. Just time for an on-the-run touch up. And a new outfit, of course.

She leaned forward and curled her upper lip down, wiping away beads of sweat but none of her lipstick. She gave her reflection a nod.

After twenty-five years as a touring singer, she couldn't begin to count the hours she'd spent in front of dressing room mirrors. The features she saw there gave her satisfaction—made up with incredible artistry by Fabia—her eyes done with a subtle cat's-eye flourish.

"We've got twelve groups for meet and greets tonight," said Teddy.

The margins on touring were tight, especially now with transport costs so high. It was never rivers of gold, but recently the diehard fans paying overs for a chance to meet her was often the difference between a tour being profitable and barely breaking even.

"Thank heavens LA is crawling with Aussies, eh?" she said to his reflection over her left shoulder in the mirror.

"There's always a good number of American fans who want meet and greets too. You're not a *complete* nobody over here."

Amber patted her forehead and grinned at her assistant's ability to deliver a sentence that was a little reassuring but full of snark. She loved

Teddy (short for Tadahisa) to death and appreciated that his Japanese sincerity and seriousness had been blunted down to a truly Aussie shit-talking dryness.

Twelve parties for meet and greets was the best number they'd had on this US tour. On a snowy night in Boise, Idaho, a couple of weeks ago, only one married couple had shown up. Amber could have talked to them much longer, but the two men had needed to head off to avoid a forecasted blizzard.

Amber had questioned whether having the last show of the tour in LA the day after Christmas would sell any tickets, but her management had talked her into it. Their argument was there were plenty of people with disposable income kicking around LA that time of year, and they would be desperate to kill the dead time between Christmas and New Year's.

She scoffed at her reflection. *Desperate souls, doing anything to kill the dead time.* Helping these people was the very point of the entertainment industry, after all. What else was any performer or creator doing?

Teddy headed for the dressing room door. "I'll give you ten minutes and then send Fabia in."

"Five will be plenty."

He nodded and closed the door behind him.

She changed into the new outfit Fabia had hung for her. Some artists who stood demurely at a mic stand for seventy minutes might be able to be within smelling distance of their fans soon afterwards, but Amber's show was high-octane. She couldn't sing her upbeat songs without bouncing around the stage—sometimes on top of a piano or a big bass drum, specially reinforced to take her weight. The new outfit was a blue spangly top and some black shorts. She wiggled in the mirror and smiled at how the spangles caught the light. The little reflections of her dressing table lights danced around the room.

There was a knock, and Fabia came in.

"I love this outfit you got me. Check this out," said Amber and spun around. "I'm a human disco ball."

Fabia laughed. "You look just like my daughter playing dress-ups. I had to give you something pretty for the last meet and greet of the tour." She gave Amber's shoulders a squeeze as she sat down in front of her at the mirror. "Beyoncé takes a team of stylists and a team of make-up-and-hair people on tour with her. You're stuck with little old me picking your outfits and clipping in your hair pieces."

Amber placed her hand over Fabia's. "I'd pick you over Beyoncé and Taylor's teams combined. And throw Miley's in there for good measure!"

Warmth flowed through Amber at the thought of the little team she had assembled around herself. Teddy, with his perfect peacocking hairdos, Fabia bringing in Tupperwares full of leftover empanadillas, and the odd assortment of bandmates and roadies she had collected. They had become her friends, and she trusted them.

When she had first moved to LA more than twenty years ago, aged nineteen with an Australian number one album under her belt, there had been plenty of people promising to propel her to superstardom, who latched onto her because they saw the potential for big dollar signs. But as the years passed, those people had fallen away, and Amber had gotten better at trusting her gut when it came to people's energy.

The energy and love of her little crew sustained her. Touring was gruelling, but as this current US tour wound to a close, she got a little pang of anticipated loneliness when she thought of her comfortable little house. There wouldn't be another person to talk to at all hours of the day or night, to start singing old Wham songs at the drop of a hat, or to fry up eggs and bacon on a camp stove on the side of the road while waiting for a tow truck for their broken-down van in the middle of Nebraska.

She'd had partners, both female and male, and had even been engaged for a period a few years back. But relationships were tough when she was on the road so much, and she had found herself single more often than not.

"There," said Fabia, placing a final touch of lipstick. "You're a picture, my love."

Amber's phone rang, and she jumped.

The country code was Australian. It was the middle of the afternoon there on a workday. Maybe a rep from her management? She pressed the button to accept the call.

"Amber, sweetie! How are you?"

A chill swept down Amber's spine and her hands went numb.

"Darling? It's Mum."

I know. The voice, which she hadn't heard in so long, froze her to the spot. She worked her throat muscles, willing herself back into action. Into a space of control. "What do you want?"

Fabia's eyebrows shot up. She spread her hands out, palms up, in an unspoken question.

Amber nodded and mouthed, *I'm fine.*

Fabia backed towards the door and made an exit, poking her face once more around the door before she closed it behind her. She looked torn, probably wondering if Amber needed privacy or a burly security guard more.

Her mother didn't miss a beat. "Just calling to see how you are, my angel. Checking in on my girl."

Amber shook her head. Her mother's tone sounded for all the world like Amber was responding to her with equal easy warmth. Like a normal daughter should. "I don't know how you got this number, but I want you to lose it. Nothing has changed. I said I didn't want any contact with you, and you need to respect that."

"Amber, if you would just—please. Listen for a—"

"I'll stop your payments if you contact me again. That was the agreement. I'm serious. I'll stop the payments."

Amber hung up and blocked the number.

She placed the phone down in front of the mirror with shaking hands.

Her shoulders sagged, and she sighed.

Someone at her Sydney management office must have slipped up. An intern or someone recently hired and wanting to please. Her mother could talk practically anyone into doing anything. It didn't matter where this security breach had come from—it was pretty much inevitable that it would happen again.

She would have to get a new American cell number. Amber couldn't block every incoming number in New South Wales.

She smiled humourlessly. Who was she kidding? The threat of the money being cut off would probably be enough to stop her darling mum trying to speak to her again.

She flung her head back. She would set Teddy to the task of changing her number—after New Years, maybe.

For now, there were more pressing matters—a line of paying customers waiting to be charmed.

She moved her mouth around to release the tension in her jaw and took a deep breath. She gave herself a last once-over in the mirror, leaning in and flicking a tiny clump of mascara off the end of an eyelash.

"The old razzle-dazzle," she said to her reflection and headed for the door.

CHAPTER 3

A young chap with trendy hair and fancy tight, red trousers led them through to the backstage area and to an old wooden corridor. Jane and Sara were at the end of the line of about twenty people. Mr Hairdo told them to wait there and he would show parties through, one by one.

Jane hid a yawn. She had come over to spend Christmas with her sister, brother-in-law, and niece and was going to house-sit and cat-sit for them for a week while they went away skiing in Whistler the following day. It was taking longer than usual to kick her jetlag from the flight from Brisbane. *When did I become middle-aged?*

Sara bounced on the balls of her feet and squealed a little under her breath. She had been in raptures about the concert they had just seen ever since Amber Hatfield bounded offstage after her encore. "I didn't even ask you—what did you think?"

Jane glanced at the line of diehard fans in front of her. Did she imagine it, or did a few shoulders tense and ears perk up, as if to hear her response? "Well," she said. Her palms were clammy. This was ridiculous! She had built a career on parsing through personal and societal biases and expressing herself clearly. She looked into her niece's expectant expression. *The truth shall set you free!* "I enjoyed it," she lied.

No, it wasn't a complete lie. It had been much too loud, and all the songs had sounded the same. Jane had been baffled when the audience screamed in recognition after hearing three notes and bellowed along with every lyric. She would not have been able to recite one line of any of the songs she had just heard, even for a million dollars.

But she had enjoyed watching Sara, grinning from ear to ear and dancing with her hands above her head. Jane wondered if she had ever, once in her life, looked as full of joy as Sara had just been for seventy solid minutes. Maybe when a new peer-reviewed research study she had contributed to was published and put in her in-tray at the university? No, that was pleasing, but it didn't make her dance.

Finally, Mr Hairdo opened a door and ushered the first party through it. A faint, musical "hello" could be heard just before the door shut again.

Sara gasped and grabbed Jane's hands. "That's her! I'm dying. I can't believe I'm going to meet Amber *Freaking* Hatfield."

Many of the other members of the queue murmured similar sentiments.

After a while, the first party, a pair of women clutching vinyl records with the covers scrawled in black Sharpie, was shown out. They made their way past the waiting fans. One was bright red in the face.

Her friend fanned her with a record. "Oh, Brandice, I'm never going to forget this night for as long as I live! Amber is an angel sent from heaven."

Jane frowned and glanced sideways at Sara. Surely these women weren't for real!

But Sara had her hand pressed to her chest and her mouth open. "Was she just the nicest?" she asked.

"Sweet as pie," said Brandice.

"And gorgeous! Didn't look a day over twenty-five, and that's a fact," said her friend.

"Enjoy, enjoy! Goodbye!" The pair waved and blew kisses to the waiting queue of fans.

Jane's head snapped up whenever another party was led out. How funny would it be if just one person, instead of gushing and swooning, reported being underwhelmed? It didn't happen, though.

She thought about all the sociology research she had read over the years about cults, groupthink, and multilevel marketing seminars where people cheered slogans in unison for hours on end. This level of agreement and harmony was often cringe-worthy, and sometimes downright dangerous.

Mary, Mary, quite contrary.

Lauren's voice echoed in her head. She shook it, like she was trying to stop the thought taking hold. Lauren had called her Mary whenever Jane was being, in Lauren's words, a grump. She had called her Mary more often than her real name in the final few months.

At last, they were the only ones left. Mr Hairdo opened the door and gestured for them to enter. Sara exhaled sharply and straightened her shoulders. She didn't move.

Jane linked her arm around her niece's and gently moved them both forward.

Inside, Amber Hatfield finished sipping on the straw of a gigantic cup with a lid and walked up to them. The cup was almost comically large for such a tiny woman.

"Hello, thank you so much for—" Sara burst into tears, and Amber wrapped her in a tight hug. "Aw, honey!"

"I–I'm sorry," Sara said between snuffles and sobs.

"Hey now, sweetie. There, there. No need to cry. You haven't been called to the principal's office to get in trouble. I'm nice, I swear." Amber rubbed Sara's back.

Jane stood with her arms hung by her sides. She wanted to step in and help in some way, but Amber had Sara all wrapped up. She locked eyes with a big man standing in the corner in a security guard's uniform, but his gaze slid away. The situation unfolding in front of him must not have been on his list of responsibilities.

Sara smiled. It was watery, but her breathing was returning to normal.

"Here. Why don't you have a little sip of water." Amber handed Sara a little half-size plastic bottle, like the ones on planes, and offered her a box of tissues.

Sara took a couple.

Jane raised her eyebrows. The room was set up like these tearful breakdowns were common, even expected. No wonder Amber had been so quick to de-escalate the situation.

"If I'm not mistaken, I detect a familiar accent?" Amber said to Jane.

Jane blinked.

Amber raised her eyebrows and cocked her head a little.

Jane wasn't the type to be starstruck easily, unless she counted that time she had met Laureate Professor Clare Figgins-Thorpe from the Australian National University after a talk on anthropological interconnectivity a few years ago. But having the woman whom she had just watched perform to screaming fans right here in front of her in a little room, looking so intently at her, created a strange dissonance that threw her a little. Plus, Amber was so...bright. Eye-catching blonde hair, all different little hints of colour on her face–even her fingernails were a loud orange. And she was wearing a shirt that shone and reflected the light. Jane had the urge to shield her eyes as if she had been dazzled, but at the same time, it was difficult to look away.

"Um, yes. We're Australian. Like you." Jane nodded. She cleared her throat, all of a sudden remembering that Amber was an actual person, so normal manners and conversational conventions applied to this very strange situation. "I'm Jane, and this is my niece, Sara." She gestured to Sara. The last thing she wanted to do was monopolise all the time at this meet and greet. Mr Hairdo was probably outside the door with an old-fashioned stopwatch, like a very overdressed swim coach.

"Sara, lovely to meet you. Do you live here in LA, or are you visiting?"

Sara's eyes went wide. Her throat muscles started working, but to no avail.

"Uh," said Jane, hoping to give her niece another minute to recover herself. "Sara and her parents live here. I'm visiting from Brisbane."

"Aw, beautiful! I love Brissie. Some great venues. I played the Fortitude Valley Music Hall this year."

There was a short silence. Sara looked at her, still with a stunned expression.

"We, uh, very much enjoyed your concert tonight. Thank you," Jane said. She was fully aware how idiotic she sounded. *Thank you?* She was talking to an internationally renowned singer, not her Uber driver.

But it was so important that this experience was a positive one for Sara, who had built it up so much in her head. If the whole conversation crashed and burned, Sara would be devastated.

"No, thank *you* for being part of such a great audience. What song did you enjoy the most?"

Now it was Jane's turn to be a deer in the headlights. Her throat muscles worked overtime, but no words came out. "Mmmmmmmm. Yep. Favourite number, hey? It would have to be... the one—the one about...the heart?" She finished this response in a pitch so high, only dogs would have heard it.

Amber pressed her lips together.

Was she annoyed?

"'The Moonlight Moves Me'." Sara's voice rang firm and clear.

"Oh, fantastic," said Amber. "That's one of my absolute favourites to perform. I wrote it with—"

"Benny Linten. The same month he was signed for his first album." Sara's words tumbled out.

Jane neck muscles loosened for the first time since they'd walked into the room.

Amber giggled. "Wow! You really know your stuff, Sara. Benny really is a sweetheart. Hey, what's your favourite song off his latest album?"

And they were off to the races. Sara was utterly charmed by her idol, like a snake in a basket in the thrall of a guy with a flute.

Jane's cheeks started to ache. She was grinning too.

Amber chatted, laughed, and took Sara by the arm. At one point, Sara asked how Amber got her ideas for songs.

Jane pressed her lips together. How many times must the singer have been asked that question?

But Amber's brows knitted, and she answered in a very genuine way, her eyes intent on Sara the whole time.

After a few minutes of chat, Sara was on a happy rolling boil. "And Jane bought the tickets for me for Christmas. You should have seen my face when they fell out of my card. My dad got a photo. She said she originally bought three, but then Lauren broke up with her, so—" She sucked air between her teeth. "Shit, sorry Jane. I didn't mean to mention Lauren."

Jane flinched. She forced a smile, although her face struggled to cooperate. "It's fine."

"Let me get Teddy back in here to take some photos!" Amber said, sounding for all the world like the idea had just occurred to her. She gave a brisk double tap on the door.

Mr Hairdo took his place at a tripod with a big camera on it.

Amber and Sara smiled as the camera clicked.

"Let's get some fun ones, Sara. Say 'LA, baby'!" Amber dragged Sara close with one arm, and they threw their other arms into the air.

"LA, baby!" Sara laughed.

Jane stood behind Mr Hairdo's shoulder to watch her niece having the time of her life.

"Get a close-up, Ted!" said Amber.

She squeezed Sara with both arms, their cheeks pressing together.

Jane shuddered inwardly. Amber was brave, getting so up-close-and-personal with complete strangers. This flu season had already been a bad one. She had a mini bottle of hand sanitizer in her pocket and a big pump bottle in the car. Hopefully Sara could be impressed upon to use a good amount of it.

"Jump in here, Jane," said Amber, waving her hand.

"Oh, no thank you," she replied, a little louder than she meant to. She was surprised Amber had remembered her name, having heard it just the once. Jane was terrible with names.

"Come on, Aunt Jane!"

"Yes, don't you want to memorialise this night forever?" Amber asked.

Amber and Sara both laughed.

Jane didn't get what was funny. She ran what they had just said in her mind but couldn't identify the joke.

Jane moved forward and stood next to her niece.

"Nope, I'm too short to be on the end. Plus, I like being the centre of attention." Amber pulled Jane by the arm and positioned her on her other side.

Amber held Jane loosely around the waist. She hung on a little tighter as Mr Hairdo asked them to say cheese.

Amber's hair was very close to Jane's face. It smelt good, something floral but not too sweet. She had expected it to smell of chemicals, like old-fashioned hairspray.

But since when had she started noticing how people's hair smelled, let along forming unsolicited preconceptions about it?

She blinked a few times. *Focus up! You're going to look in these photos like a confused stranger who wandered in off the street.* "Cheese."

"Perfect!" said Amber.

When the photos were done, including some selfies on Sara's phone (she couldn't possibly wait the twelve hours until the email came through with all Mr Hairdo's photos attached), they said their goodbyes. Sara and Amber hugged like old friends at an airport.

Mr Hairdo pointed them down the corridor towards the exit.

"Can you even?" Sara said.

Jane wasn't sure what this meant or how to respond, so she stayed silent.

"Amber is a dream. My hands are still shaking. I need to splash some water on my face. And pee. Not at the same time, though. You know what I mean."

Sara ducked through a dark-green door into the loos.

Jane looked up at the ceiling of the El Rey Theatre hallway. A modern smoke detector flashed its little blipping light, but otherwise the woodwork, and even the dark-maroon paint, could have been original.

Jane yawned. The absence of Sara was also the absence of the excited energy that had carried Jane through the long evening. And Sara would be leaving for longer the next day. *More time alone.* The days stretched out grey and empty in front of her.

"Excuse me."

Jane started.

Mr Hairdo had snuck up and was standing right beside her. His bright-orange sneakers had masked the sound of his approach.

"Sorry, sorry. Amber asked me to give this to you." He handed her a folded piece of lined paper.

"Oh, um, my niece already got an autograph."

He winced. "No, uh, this is not for your niece. It's for you. Thank you." He walked a few steps backwards, then turned tail and hurried away.

Jane narrowed her eyes as he retreated. *Very strange behaviour.* There was a lot about this unusual evening that put her off kilter.

She unfolded the scrap of paper. The top had the little bits still on it, where it had been ripped from a notepad.

In deep purple pen was written: *Amber Hatfield.* Followed by a series of digits that looked like an American cell phone number.

Jane narrowed her eyes so much, her vision went grey.

CHAPTER 4

Jane's phone buzzed and rang in the middle of the big kitchen-island bench.

"No caller ID," said Sara, craning her neck to see the screen.

"Probably some robo-scam," said Jane's brother-in-law, Bill, his mouth full of Cinnamon Toast Crunch and milk.

"Screen it, I reckon," said her sister Barbara.

Jane screwed up her nose. The pop singer's phone number was burning a hole in her bedside table drawer upstairs. There was no way she had tracked down Jane's contact details with secret technology that only famous people had access to—was there? There was a lot about this city Jane didn't know.

The phone pealed and vibrated some more. Jane shook her hands next to her head then grabbed the phone and hit the green button. "Hello?"

"Hi. Jane? It's Lauren."

Sara, who was sitting closest to Jane, let out a groan. She mouthed Lauren's name to her parents, and they both groaned as well.

"Have I caught you at an inopportune time? Are you at some kind of farm?" Lauren asked.

A tiny muscle twitched next to Jane's right eye. The musical English-accented voice in her ear had not so long ago been the soundtrack that ran through her mind. Her therapist had set her an exercise to write down everything that voice said to her in a constant loop late at night, and burn it.

"No. What can I help you with?"

"Oh, straight to it, I see. Well, it's Wordsworth, I need to take him to the vet."

Jane stomach plummeted. They had gotten the Cavalier King Charles Spaniel as a puppy eight years before. He now lived with Lauren. Jane didn't have any visitation rights because Lauren said seeing her again would confuse him and set off his anxiety. "Is he OK? What's going on?"

Sara mouthed *Wordsworth* to Barbara and Bill, and they looked at each other wide-eyed. Sara rubbed Jane's back with a firm hand.

"I need the pet insurance policy number," Lauren said. "Do you have it?"

"No, I, uh..." Jane put her hand to her throat. Her face was hot.

"We agreed you would continue to pay for the policy," Lauren said. "You have been making the payments, haven't you? We agreed. I'm bearing the cost of all his food and grooming."

"No, I mean, yes, I've set up a direct debit. It's all taken care of. But I don't have the policy documents with me. I'm in LA. They were in one of the boxes I dropped off at your lawyer's chambers. What's wrong with Wordsworth?"

Lauren sighed. "He's fine. I'm taking him to get his teeth cleaned next week. I just couldn't put my hand on the insurance card. It's hard for me to go through your boxes, you see? It's painful."

Sara groaned.

Jane stalked out to the deck to let Sara reassure her parents about the health of Jane's former dog.

The wintry morning air was bracing. "Jesus Christ, Lauren. I thought there was some emergency! Isn't it midnight over there?"

Lauren drew a shuddering breath. "Don't shout at me, Jane. You know how it triggers me."

Jane put the phone on mute and let out a wordless "ahhhh-hhhh" of frustration, startling two sparrows that flew from a shrub and up into the sky with a flurry of tiny wings. Jane watched them as they rose, trying to slow her breathing.

She put the phone back to her ear. *Time to extricate myself without sustaining any further damage.*

"... anything of you without you flying off the handle. It's not the easiest thing, you know. I never thought I would be looking after him by myself. I know you left, but I hope you still have some concern for Wordsworth's welfare."

Left. The word still stung. Sure, Jane had moved out, but only after Lauren had ended it and asked her to leave. "Lauren—"

"I built my life around you, and I'm sorry if I don't have every aspect organised to within an inch of its life. Not everyone can pick up the pieces so quickly, you see? Not everyone can compartmentalise."

"Look—"

Lauren's voice went up in pitch and wavered. "I'm sorry I've interrupted your Los Angeles holiday. I, well, I thought you wouldn't mind helping me. Hello? Are you still there?"

"Shit." She still had the phone on mute. She fumbled to tap the button. "The policy details are in one of the boxes. Goodbye." She hung up and slumped down onto a wooden sun lounge. The slats were like ice against the backs of her thighs. She pressed her fingertips to her eyebrows and massaged her head.

The sliding door opened, and Sara peeked her head out. "Jane? We have to leave for the airport in ten minutes. Are you OK?"

Jane stood. "Yes, sweetie, I'm fine." She put her arm around Sara's shoulders.

Sara hugged her aunt around the middle. "Are you sure?"

"Yes, well, I'm relatively unscathed. I'm toughening up, I suppose."

"Just don't get too tough. Not everyone is like Lauren. Some people out there are nice and normal and not servants of pure evil."

Jane smiled, although she didn't feel like it. "Thank you. I'll try to remember that."

"Now, you'd better come back inside. Your toes have turned blue."

She sat back down at the kitchen island.

Barbara stood and put her arm around her. "Put the kettle on, will you, Bill?"

Jane leant against her sister and sighed.

Barbara was six years older and had fallen into the role of the "little mother" for Jane a lot when they were growing up, picking up on social cues that Jane sometimes missed and gently steering her in the right direction. She had turned a knack for minimising potential interpersonal issues into a lucrative career and was now an in-demand HR and corporate conflict-resolution consultant.

Barbara cradled Jane's head in her arms for a second, then sat on a stool next to her. "Are you sure you're going to be OK here? I feel like we shouldn't leave you alone so soon after Christmas. We can reschedule the ski trip if you need us to stay."

Bill's hand wobbled as he put Jane's cuppa down. He replaced an aghast expression with one of compassionate understanding.

Jane sat up straight. "No, don't be silly. The break-up is ancient history. It's time I stopped going to water whenever Lauren feels the urge to get in touch with me. I'll be fine here. I've got a pile of new research to read before the semester starts up." She took a sip of tea and started to feel a fraction better, as if what she was saying were true. "Plus, I won't be alone. I'll have the cat. Now, go and pack. It's almost time to go to the airport."

"Hey, come here." Barbara dragged her up by her armpits and wrapped her in a hug. "You're bullshitting the hell out of me right now, but I know how strong you are. You're going to be OK. I love you."

Jane rested her cheek against her sister's hair, breathing in comfort while she had the chance. "I love you too. And I am going to be OK."

She had been putting one foot in front of the other for so long, it had to lead to "OK" in the end. *Or else, where am I going?*

"You need to spread her wet food out in little bits around her dish."

"Why?" Jane asked. "Does she like to pretend she's in an overpriced restaurant where smears of different mashed veggies cost sixty-five dollars?"

Sara snorted from the back seat.

Barbara scoffed. "No. If it's in a big pile, she eats it too fast, then spews it up."

"Lovely," said Jane. She pulled her car into the drop-off area at LAX and put on her hazard lights.

Bill jumped out and ran to the car boot to grab everyone's big suitcases.

Jane looked into her wing mirror for the slightest break in the traffic flying by, then dashed out of the car onto the relative safety of the footpath.

Barbara wrapped her up in a hug. "The cat's completely neurotic, but she'll be well-behaved for you. I think you'll have a steadying influence on her."

"I don't know about that." Jane flinched as a minibus honked its horn, managing to be louder than the dozens of other vehicles honking at the same time; they were like a deranged choir of geese.

"You just need to stop answering calls from hidden numbers," Bill said.

"Yes, good tip. Thank you."

Her sister's family stood there, cool as cucumbers, seeming not to notice the chaos of cars and buses stopped at crazy angles behind them, or speeding around trying to gain entry.

Barbara and Bill had split their time between LA and Brisbane since they'd gotten married decades before, and had lived stateside full-time since Sara finished high school and enrolled in a psychology degree at the University of Southern California. All three of them seemed to have a shiny, hardened shell around them.

Maybe I'll develop my shell if I spend enough time in this insane metropolis.

"Remember Selena's kitty Valium is top right in your bathroom cabinet. Give her half a pill if her hair starts coming out in big clumps," said Barbara.

"Or if she forgets how to use her litter tray and wees on the floor," Sara added.

"I didn't know this house-sitting gig would involve quite so much cleaning up of excrement." Jane hugged Sara and her brother-in-law. "Have the most wonderful time. Message me when you land."

Barbara held onto her for longer than an airport hug was meant to go for.

Jane was eventually able to disentangle herself, but her sister grabbed onto her hand at the last minute.

"I can be on the first flight home if you need me," Barbara said.

"All I need you to do is enjoy this trip. You've worked so hard this year. Promise me you won't worry."

"I promise you I will try not to worry."

Jane smiled. "Good enough."

Sara ducked back for one more hug. "Thank you so much for taking me to the show last night. It was a dream come true. Amber was the best Christmas present ever."

"You're welcome, my love. Now, best go or you'll miss your flight." Jane's stomach plunged as her family walked off, wheeling big suitcases and turning back every so often to wave. It wasn't because she was going to miss them too badly but because now that the hustle and bustle of getting them to the airport was done, her mind was free to tumble back into the maddening loop of thoughts she'd been spinning all day.

Plus, Lauren had made everything worse. She could imagine Sara saying *as usual!* This lightened her mood for a few seconds.

Jane risked life, limb, and sanity by hurrying back out into the traffic and jumping in her car by the driver's-side door. Her adrenaline and cortisol spiked as she pulled back out into the LAX traffic and didn't start to level out again until she was off the I-105 and back on the surface streets of Silver Lake.

She exhaled slowly, loosening her grip on the wheel. A knotty thought hit her again.

Amber Hatfield.

Why had the strange, sparkly woman given Jane her phone number? She seemed like the kind of person who did a lot of things on whims. Jane didn't like whims. They had an uncomfortable way of turning well-ordered worlds upside-down.

A tension headache built in her temple. She shook her head and rolled her shoulders.

She hadn't slept well the night before. She always tried to get at least seven and a half hours of good-quality sleep but had tossed and turned.

Jane took a deep breath. She always felt better when she could follow a problem down a line of logic to the solution.

So what's the problem?

She couldn't decide whether to contact Amber Hatfield. And the uncertainty was tying her stomach up in knots and making her brain fuzzy.

Amber must have given Jane her number because there was some other meet and greet add-on she was able to offer Sara. She couldn't even begin to imagine what it could possibly be. Once at the university, another staff member had been given a short video message from a retired football player by his grandchildren for his birthday. Her colleague had been thrilled.

Jane frowned again now, baffled by what some people liked.

A text message was the best option. She would send a text and never receive a reply. This would annoy her, as it got to the heart of two of her pet peeves—loose ends left untied and people being inconsiderate. It really wasn't worth it.

Better than a call, though. Jane grimaced. She imagined the dial tone trilling on and on in her ear, then being abruptly commanded to leave a voicemail. Or worse, a ten-second message that would be converted to text! An arbitrary time limit, plus the added indignity of having your remarks converted by a computer. The possibility for ambiguity and confusion was too much to handle.

Or *even* worse, if Amber answered, in the middle of a facial treatment with cucumbers on her eyes. Or on a red carpet doing that pose women do where they stick one leg forward, cameras flashing all around her?

Jane supposed, on second thought, it was probably not usual to hold a red carpet at 10:48 in the morning—but this *was* Hollywood, after all.

The headache got stronger.

There was a possibility of a result that would benefit Sara, so she had to do something. She couldn't get to the bottom of why this whole situation was spinning her out so much. There was only one way to get to the end of it.

She turned right into the parking lot of a Jack in the Box fast-food restaurant. She parked, fumbled for her phone, and pulled the slip of paper out of her jeans pocket.

She squared her shoulders as she keyed the number into her phone and typed up a text message.

Hello, Amber. It's Jane here from yesterday evening's meet and greet. You gave me your number, so I am following up. What can I do for you? Regards.

The text bubble turned green as she hit send.

There. She had done her due diligence for her niece. It would be annoying to have the unanswered text sit there on her phone, but she would cope. Jane exhaled and relaxed back into her seat a little.

Her phone pealed its beeping ringtone and started to buzz.

She dropped it, tried to retrieve it out of midair, then fumbled it onto the floor on the passenger side. She reached down to grab it but went too quick—the seatbelt engaged, and she jerked backwards, pain shooting through her chest.

"Bloody stinking hell!" She tried again, slower this time. She stretched across and down. Her fingers scrabbled for the phone. She made a last mini-lunge, but the seatbelt engaged again.

"Bastard bleeding damnation!" She unclicked the seatbelt, fell forward and did a half roll onto the passenger seat. During this maneuver, she managed to grab her phone and hit the green circle.

"Hello?" Jane said. She tried to shift onto her back, but her metal water bottle caught her between the shoulder blades. "Gah!"

"Hi?" said the voice through the phone. "It's Amber here. Amber Hatfield. Have I, uh, caught you at a bad time?"

Jane looked upwards out the passenger window at the cloudless LA winter sky. "No, I, uh, no, it's as good a time as any." She heaved herself upright as silently as she could. Sitting back in the driver's seat, she smoothed her hair.

"Well, thank you for texting me. I wasn't sure you would."

Jane narrowed her eyes, not sure how to respond. She had expected Amber to launch into a spiel about a special signed mascara bottle she wanted to offer to Sara, or a vinyl record with the cover made entirely of magenta feathers. "You're welcome."

"Thanks, I..."

There was a pause. Jane pursed her lips. She was damned if she was going to say "you're welcome" again.

"Look," Amber continued. "I've got a few days free coming up. I was wondering if you would like to, maybe, meet up? Maybe do some LA things, since you said you're visiting."

Jane frowned, really flummoxed now. "Do you mean Sara? She's gone on a family trip to the snow."

"No, I didn't mean Sara. I meant you."

Jane slumped into her seat. Granted, she didn't know much about celebrity meet and greets, but she was pretty sure this type of invitation was not a usual element of them.

"Are you free tomorrow?" Amber asked.

No, I'm busy. Goodbye forever, you strange woman. Jane was about to gladly extricate herself from this confusing conversation. But she stopped. She had been a researcher for many years, and one of her great joys was considering a question and really diving in to get to the bottom of it.

Was she free tomorrow? She had to feed Selena the cat in the morning and at night. Other than that, she had planned to read a little and go for a walk around her sister's neighbourhood. If there was somewhere that looked nice for lunch, maybe she would stop in. Read some more. Try not to think about Lauren.

"Yes, I am free tomorrow," Jane said. Adhering to Selena's schedule was important, but it didn't count as "plans."

"Oh, great. Let's meet for coffee in the arvo and go from there? I'll text you the address of a nice place I know. Sara said you're in Silver Lake."

Jane's thoughts were all a jumble. It was considerate of Amber to remember so much about her. Or was this level of recall off-putting? No, it was nice when people were accommodating. "OK," she said.

"Awesome! I'll text you soon with the deets. See you tomorrow."

"Goodbye."

The silence inside the car was loud. A feeling of unreality settled on Jane. Had that really just happened? Maybe she had hit her head against the glovebox a minute ago and had a very realistic hallucination.

She cracked the window to let some air in. The Jack in the Box car park that had been nearly empty when she arrived was now about half full. The bustle of car doors being opened and shut, and music being played somewhere nearby, calmed her.

Another research question lodged itself into her brain. *What on earth was going on?*

For starters, her headache was gone. She rubbed her neck, wondering if she had sustained mild whiplash. She had made an early New Year's resolution to get out of her comfort zone more, but she hadn't intended to cause herself physical injury.

She looked at her watch. About twenty-eight hours to mull it all over before she was due to meet Amber Hatfield for coffee, and "go from there." *Whatever the hell that means.*

CHAPTER 5

"You really don't have to drive me. I can get a Lyft," said Amber.

Teddy pulled the car door shut. "Nonsense. I'm happy to chauffeur. I can add it to my resume for when you kick me to the curb and I need to find another B-list celebrity who needs an assistant."

Amber gave his arm a playful slap. "I know you're trying to give me shit, but 'B-list?' I'm stoked with that. Surely I'm actually more like F-list."

He laughed as he started the car. "Or P-list. How far down the alphabet do the lists go?"

"Oh, har har. Add 'comedian' to your resume." She looked out the car window at the Santa Monica footpath.

"Just be glad you never made it to A-list. You wouldn't be going to meet a complete stranger in a public place without a full security detail and tactical snipers on every surrounding rooftop."

"True, true. But Jane isn't a *complete* stranger. We've both met her."

Amber glanced sideways at Teddy, who kept his eyes on the road ahead.

"What?" Amber asked. "What is that non-reaction?"

Teddy puffed out his cheeks. "Just that, babe. A non-reaction. Look, I was just very surprised that you've made this date. I was there for most of the time you spent with her. Unless she was a completely different person when you and her and the niece were together without me, I'm just not sure, well, what she gave you. You know, that warranted me rushing out to give her your number? It's not like you do that kind of thing lightly."

"What do you mean? Are you saying I usually have three months of flirting, then a six-month emotional affair with someone before I ask them out on a first date?"

Teddy scoffed. "Yeah, something like that. Or exactly that."

"And how does that usually work out for me?"

He took one hand off the wheel to mime something plummeting and crashing into the earth, complete with sound effects.

Amber smiled. "Geez, don't hold back or anything, Ted."

"Sorry."

"The definition of madness is doing something over and over and expecting a different result. I thought I'd mix it up."

Teddy wrinkled his nose. "So this is some kind of social experiment?"

Amber sighed. *What was it?* Not a social experiment. Something new, though. But was it a good idea? Her insides were swishing around uncomfortably, so maybe not. "I met someone new, thought she was hot, took a big swing. I might clear the rope or lose middle stump."

"Huh?"

"Sorry, cricket reference."

"I was in the baseball club in elementary school in Japan, but I'll never understand cricket."

"Awwww, you were? You would have been so cute in your little knickerbockers! And here was me thinking you're allergic to all sports."

"Quit changing the subject."

Amber scowled. "OK, OK. So, what is it? You think I've gone nuts? Would you find it so hard to believe I'm not insane if Jane looked like, I dunno, Jessica Alba?"

"Whoa, whoa, whoa. First of all, who is Jessica Alba? And second of all, Jane being hot is not up for debate. Jane is a smoke show. Tall, dark, and handsome? Break me off a piece!"

"We've talked about this, Teddy. A big part of your job is to pretend to get my Elder Millennial references. If you make me feel old, I'll go full diva on you."

Teddy sucked air in through his teeth. "Oh. God. No. Let me try that again. Jane is easily as hot as Jessica Alba, the...Italian tennis player?"

"Bah-bow." Amber did her best impression of a wrong guess on *Wheel of Fortune.*

"Gah!" He gripped the wheel tightly with both hands. "I give up! On all of it. You're a grown woman—"

"And then some!"

He ignored her and ploughed on. "And you can give your number to however many sexy, awkward women you like."

Amber bowed with a flourish. "Oh, thank you. How kind. I appreciate that and intend to take full advantage."

Teddy chuckled and shook his head.

Amber watched Culver City fly past the window. Her guts felt like they were being squeezed by a boa constrictor. She took a deep breath, telling herself it was normal to be nervous for a date. Teddy was right—she never put herself out there this quick.

Was sending Teddy to chase Jane down with her number a moment of madness? She pictured Jane when she had first walked into the meet and greet. Even now, she smiled out at the footpath. Jane had been the picture of a fish out of water. Looking around like the backstage area of a pop concert was as strange as the surface of Mars.

Amber had had to bite her lip to stop from laughing out loud. She hadn't been able to help herself and teased Jane a little, quizzing her about her favourite song of the night. It was something she never, ever did. Usually the ease and comfort of fans generous enough to pay for a ticket, let alone the cost of a meet and greet, was of utmost importance to her.

But something had made her want to push Jane. Get a reaction out of her. Make her sweat.

And what had been revealed was how much Jane loved her niece. Amber could see how hard it was for Jane to smooth over an awkward situation while her niece floundered. But she had kept on. And the look of pure joy she had when Sara had started to enjoy herself shone.

When Jane left, Amber had felt her absence like a little chill in the air. So she had grabbed a pen and sent Teddy on a chase, thinking there was about a zero per cent chance of Jane actually getting in contact with her.

When the text had come through like a formal reply to a tax audit notice, Amber had hit the call button right away. Jane on the phone had been just the same as Jane in person. Genuine to the core. No schmooze or bullshit. Amber had felt like an absolute nutter proposing they spend the afternoon together and had nearly fallen off the couch when Jane said yes.

"What do you think Jane does for a living?" she blurted to Teddy as they neared their destination. "Librarian?"

"Hmmmm. Sexy professor? Supreme Court judge? Vegas showgirl?"

Amber scoffed. Teddy was trying to ease her nerves by being stupid. She appreciated him for it.

The GPS told them their destination was just ahead on the right. Her insides jolted. *Time to put your money where your mouth is, Hatfield.*

CHAPTER 6

Jane hadn't meant to be early, but she was on her third glass of café tap water. A lecturer she had once worked with had called her "offensively punctual". But did early count as punctual or only being right on time? She pulled out her phone to consult the Oxford Dictionary online but caught sight of Mr Hairdo and Amber Hatfield outside the big front window. Jane was struck by how normal Amber looked.

She winced a little at herself. It had been silly to expect her be walking down the street in a shiny stage costume. Amber's hair looked less, well, big, and her jeans, T-shirt, and jacket weren't in the least bit eye-catching. She looked great, though. How did some people just wear clothes well—look put-together and confident? She never did.

Amber spotted Jane and waved. Jane automatically raised her hand in return, stiffly with her fingers splayed. She hurried to put it down again. A few people glanced at Amber then at her. Did they recognise Amber, or were they just subconsciously moved to be interested in her and what she was doing? Amber was kind of magnetic like that.

Mr Hairdo had a good look around the café, leant to say something to Amber, then squeezed her arm and left.

A server rushed to meet Amber at the door. They hadn't done that to Jane. Amber smiled, motioned with both hands towards Jane, and said, "I'm meeting someone."

Warmth rose in Jane's chest. She went to fix her hair but gripped the edge of the table to keep her hands in place. She was being ridiculous.

Over the course of another restless night and troubled morning, she had settled even more firmly on the conclusion that Amber was flighty. One of those people who threw their actions out into the universe with no forethought. Just for fun. She probably spent all kinds of afternoons with all kinds of odds-and-ends people she picked up along the way. Ended up at her interior designer's baby shower, that sort of thing.

Jane wasn't going to be sucked in.

Yet, despite her strongest resolutions, Jane smiled as Amber crashed down into the seat opposite her.

"Oof. Sorry I'm late, Jane. It's great to see you. Thanks for coming."

Jane noted how Amber used her name right away. A tactic designed to charm. She had read somewhere that Bill Clinton did it all the time. And, in hindsight, he had been a bit sleazy. "You're not late at all, *Amber.* I got here early. I left plenty of time in case the traffic was bad."

"Oh, smart. LA traffic is the pits."

"Yes."

A server asked Amber what type of water she wanted. The answer was tap.

"Isn't it so funny how there are five choices of water here? There's only ever a maximum of two in Australia," said Amber.

Jane considered. "Yes, that is a noticeable difference. You could put it down to America's consumer culture. And the tip economy. Here they bend over backwards to make the customer happy."

Amber smiled.

Jane's insides sank. She was talking too much again. If Amber were less polite, her eyes would have been glazing over. They looked bright with interest, though. A deep blue, like a sapphire in sunlight. Jane pressed her lips together. Amber was a great pretender.

"Sorry," said Jane. "I'm not much of a chatter. I've been told I say too much or not enough."

Amber's bright eyes widened. She opened her mouth, but the conscientious server loomed over them again.

"Ready to order?"

"Yes, I'll have a tea, please," said Jane.

"Wonderful! Iced, with oat milk, lemon, sugar, or peach infusion?"

"Errr, boiling please. Just, um, water and leaves in a cup."

Amber let out a spluttering cough. She cleared her throat. "I'll have a coffee please. Just water and beans."

The server creased her forehead but still beamed. "Perfect! I'll have those right out."

Jane wanted to sink into the floor. She couldn't even order a cup of tea like a normal human being. She didn't know what Amber hoped to get out of this little tete-a-tete, but she was sure Amber now wanted to stand up and walk out of there quick smart.

That's it. Jane clamped her mouth shut and resolved to get through this weird interaction with the minimum of embarrassment. The only way she was going to was to speak as little as possible.

"You know what I think?" Amber asked.

That you have massive regrets about meeting up with me today? Jane shook her head, her lips still closed.

"Chatting is way overrated. Like, we could have chatted easily back and forth about the water thing—'Totally, twelve dollars for Perrier fizzy water? Get outta here!'— and ninety-nine times out of one hundred, people here who are good chatters have a thousand thoughts running through their heads while they're talking to you. Maybe I've been in LA too long, but often it seems like they're thinking about what they can get out of an interaction—exposure, media capital, opportunities.

"But when you were talking about the water just now, it seemed like you were really talking about the water."

"Plus the US 'customer is king' culture."

Amber grinned. "That too. Plus the ingredients of a cup of tea."

Jane relaxed her mouth enough to smile. "If I get a steaming cup of water with shrub leaves floating in it, I really only have myself to blame. Good tea is an elusive thing in this country. Most people don't even own kettles."

"Mine's going to have whole coffee beans bobbing around in it. Oop, here she comes."

Jane's insides untangled as Amber smiled up at the server, who put down two very normal-looking hot beverages and bid her retreat.

So what if Amber charmed people en masse for a living? Jane was enjoying a social interaction with someone who wasn't a family member for the first time in a long time. Since her relationship had gone down in a blazing—

"Who told you you were bad at chatting?" Amber asked.

"Lauren." The answer came quickly. "My, uh, my ex."

"Oh."

Jane glanced up from her tea.

Amber's eyes were narrowed slightly.

The silence stretched. Jane cast around for something to say. "She was my colleague at the university. Well, still is my colleague, actually."

"University. Are you a professor?" Amber cleared her throat again.

"No, senior lecturer. I actually may have the opportunity to be promoted to associate professor at the end of next semester." Heavy anxiety thudded into her chest. This whole crazy café situation was meant to be a distraction from Lauren and potential promotion, but now she had mentioned both within a minute.

"Cool! What does that process involve?"

"Oh, um, do you really want to know? There are a lot of steps." Jane's stomach jolted like she'd stepped in the pothole. "Shit, I don't mean you wouldn't be able to understand it. It's just very, very boring to most people." She winced.

Amber took a sip of her coffee. "Jane, as long as you don't tell me about Spotify streams, social media strategies, or tour itineraries, I promise you that whatever you tell me will be the most interesting thing in the world to me at this moment. I want to hear what you lecture about too."

Jane tried to hide a half-smile. She was being charmed. *But so what?* It felt good. She would never see this pretty, amusing woman after today, but being listened to and smiled at was a nice break from the thudding anxiety and solitude that had become her existence lately.

She shifted a little to get comfier in her chair and planted her feet. "The candidates for the associate professorship will be evaluated for three key attributes—recognition, distinction, and leadership." She took a sip of tea.

"Oh, wow. So, recognition. Is that you recognising things or being recognised for things?"

Jane explained it was the latter and launched into a list of research or other academic outcomes that could qualify.

As she warmed up, she leant forward.

Amber did as well.

Those eyes, trained on her with focus and attention, really were very blue.

CHAPTER 7

"My car's parked a couple of blocks away," said Jane.

They were out the front of the café. Amber had tried to pay the bill for both of them, but Jane insisted on splitting it.

"Oh," said Amber. She cast around for something else to say. Now that Jane's departure was imminent, a faint panic rose in her chest. "You were lucky to get a park so close. Street parking around here can be a challenge. The residents complain about it."

"Yes. My sister has enough garage space, so it's not an issue for her."

Amber took a breath and tried to gather herself. Sure, she had big feelings about most things. It often drove the people around her crazy. But this feeling of wanting to keep Jane close to her was a bit over the top, even for her. The woman was a stranger.

A stranger with a smile that she didn't give away to just anyone. But the few times Amber had gotten to see Jane smile—watching her niece at the meet and greet, and this afternoon—it had been beautiful. Precious.

While they had been sitting and chatting, the rest of the world outside the confines of their little table had fallen away. There was only them. Amber had felt a calmness that was rare for her.

Jane had told her about her anthropology and sociology studies. Sharing how much she enjoyed teaching her uni students and getting into knotty discussions with them had produced a particularly lovely smile.

"Excuse me, I'm so sorry," a voice said.

Amber flinched. She knew that tone, and she knew what was coming. She plastered a smile on her face before she turned towards the voice.

The voice belonged to a woman with short hair, in her mid-thirties. "I hate to interrupt, but are you Amber Hatfield?"

"Guilty as charged," Amber replied.

The woman gasped. "I knew it! I just had to come over. I'm visiting from Iowa, and I bet my sister back home that I would see a real-life celebrity in Hollywood. I'm such a huge fan. Your album *Burn the Sun* was huge for me, you know, when I was coming out."

"That is so sweet! What's your name?"

"Della."

"Della. You've made my day. Can I give you a hug?"

Della beamed and nodded.

"Let's get a picture so you can win that bet with your sister. Although I'm not sure I count as a celebrity. If you head down further down Sunset Boulevard, I'm sure you'll see half a dozen Elvises and a handful of Michael Jacksons."

Della laughed and pulled out her phone.

"I can take a picture," said Jane.

"Oh, Jane. Are you sure?" Amber didn't want to make Jane feel like part of her entourage. She tried to read Jane's face.

"Of course."

"Thank you," said Della. "I'm terrible at selfies." She handed Jane her phone.

"Say cheese," said Jane. She took a few snaps, then stepped in closer and took a couple more.

After another hug, Della took her leave. She looked Jane up and down before she walked away.

Amber had the anxious idea that she would ask Jane who she was and what she was doing there. She smiled again and gave Della a last wave. She had seemed pretty normal—no reason to think she would start interrogating Amber's date. If Jane even knew it was a date.

"Does that happen a lot?" asked Jane.

"Well, every so often, I guess. Sorry." She *was* sorry, for letting Jane stand there ignored while she turned on the charm with a stranger.

"Don't be sorry. That lady was very appreciative. Well, my car is this way."

Amber's insides shrivelled. *She's annoyed at being interrupted and is brushing me off.* Amber should have handled the whole thing a lot better.

"I feel a bit amped from all those leaves in the hot water," Jane continued. "Would you want to walk the long way round with me?"

Relief flooded through Amber. She tried to stifle a beaming grin but couldn't.

"That sounds absolutely amazing."

They fell into step side-by-side. Walking next to Jane was comfortable. Weirdly so. Like Amber's body recognised Jane as an old friend she had walked beside thousands of times.

She snuck a sideways look. Jane strode, her arms swinging. Amber had to pick up the pace for her shorter legs to keep up. She smiled again.

"I've always preferred being on the move. Even when I was a kid," Amber said.

"Me too. Do you ever get tired of being approached out of the blue like that?"

Amber knitted her eyebrows. "Yeah, sometimes. Della was kind of an A-plus interaction, though. I was just worried I was being rude to you."

"You weren't rude. I didn't mind. What was A-plus about the interaction?"

Amber decided to believe Jane. She wasn't mad. She had told her so. She didn't wear her heart on her sleeve like other people Amber knew, but she trusted in what Jane said. *Kind of weird to trust a stranger so quickly. Maybe it wouldn't hurt to keep my guard up a tiny bit.*

They turned up a street lined with cute bungalows ranging in colour from white to a faded terracotta. She took a deep breath of the crisp air and decided her guard could go to hell. "First of all, Della didn't yell. When she came up and spoke to us. To the people around us, it probably appeared like a normal conversation. But I've had people yell, and that can draw a crowd. Especially here in LA. When a commotion starts up, people automatically think Julia Roberts has shown up and started signing autographs. Airports are the worst because people are usually bored. They sometimes start jostling and taking photos even if they don't know who I am."

"I wouldn't like that. Do you travel with security?"

Amber chuckled. "No, I'm way too small-time for that. There was a time back when I was a teenager and my album hit number one in Australia—the label arranged for security to go everywhere with me. A nice guy named Goran. But here in the States, many years past the height of my fame, I can get away with living a pretty normal life."

"Do you ever think twice about going places, like the café today?" She paused. "Oh, look, that little park looks nice. Should we head in there?"

"Good idea. I don't worry here in the US. It's a needle-in-a-haystack chance that someone will recognise me here. Della's actually a very rare case—a homegrown US fan. Mostly when someone clocks me here, it's another Aussie.

"It's one of the reasons I don't go home as often as I should. In Australia, I need security with me for most public appearances—anything where I'm out and about as 'Amber Hatfield'. On a trip to the corner shop to get milk, I can usually wear big sunglasses and a beanie and not be recognised. But any outing bigger than that can go sideways pretty quickly."

Jane nodded.

Amber had painted a sad picture; she knew that. She was sort of an exile. Flashes from when things had "gone sideways" flashed through her brain. She could have said a lot more, but she didn't want to dredge up past traumas when the afternoon was so beautiful and serene.

She looked up, taking in the dense deep-green foliage of the benjamin figs that formed a natural arch overhead. They were alone in their little shady section of the park.

"It's a bit chilly here in the shade. Nice and fresh, though," said Jane.

Amber slowed and looked up also. "I'll have to remember this place. In summer, LA sometimes feels like there's not one bit of shade in the whole city—just unrelenting sun."

A breeze picked up and made all the little leaves rustle and hiss. Dappled spots of sunlight danced over her and Jane.

Amber's heart leapt at the unexpected natural beauty of it all. It was like the two of them had been removed from the bustling, bright city to this eerie yet comfortable place.

She grinned and ran the knuckle of her index finger across the exposed skin of Jane's wrist, where it stuck out of her jacket arm. "You've got goosebumps," she said.

Amber shivered. She looked at Jane. She imagined kissing her mouth, how it would be warm. Jane's arms around her would be soft yet strong. She pictured it all so clearly—she thought for a second she'd actually done it.

Amber hadn't known her long, but she knew Jane was deliberate and thoughtful. What would it be like to kiss someone like that? *I want to find out!*

Jane rubbed her wrist, like she'd just had a handcuff removed. Her brow furrowed, like a dark cloud scudding across a clear sky.

Amber's cheeks burned. *Ah shit, I've made her uncomfortable now. Stupid, stupid! Why do I have to act on every impulse that pops into my head?*

Her mind raced. What was her play here? She wanted to take things further with Jane, ask her out to a candlelit dinner, take her home afterwards to a bed strewn with rose petals.

Every impulse told her to take a big swing.

But the risk of being rejected was too much. She needed *something*, some sign that Jane wasn't just a very polite, uninterested aunt of one of her fans. *I just need more time with her.*

"So I know you've spent a lot of time in LA visiting your family, but have you had the full cheesy, tacky tourist experience? Like, way over the top? Have you done the Hollywood Walk of Fame?"

"Yes, I believe I've had that full experience. I went to see Britney Spears' star with Sara when she was ten. We got ice cream sundaes afterwards, and they had a flavour called Cookie Monster that was bright blue."

Aw. Amber melted at how well Jane remembered her day out with her niece. Her lips pursed as she pictured Jane taking photo after photo of little Sara crouching and posing on the footpath. "I'm assuming it was your idea to go and pay homage to Britney?"

"Me? Oh, no. Sara was going through a big phase at that age. I must have sat through that *Crossroads* movie half a dozen times. Wait, you're joking aren't you?"

"Just a little. Do you mind?"

Jane frowned, and her eyes fixed on a point beyond Amber's shoulder. She was silent.

Amber counted two breaths. *Three, four, five.*

"I don't mind." Jane looked right into Amber's eyes again. "Your teasing is like Sara's. My friends at work don't joke very often, and my ex would say things that weren't the truth, but in a different way. That would make me feel like the ground was always shifting about.

"I was diagnosed with autism spectrum disorder about four years ago," she continued. "It means I don't read social cues well, and it's difficult sometimes to jump from one train of thought to another. I can fall off the edge of a conversation quite quickly. Lauren would say, 'Keep up! You want people to still think you're smart', things like that."

Amber swallowed with an effort. Her throat was thick. The one-two punch of Jane giving *such* serious thought to her question, being so open about her neurodivergence, then being vulnerable about being hurt in the past, had set a burning desire running up her body. *Uh-oh! I promised my therapist I wouldn't pick up any more birds with broken wings.*

Sara had let slip that Jane had an ex, maybe a recent one, and Jane had mentioned her too. *Lauren.* The name had stuck in Amber's head.

Maybe I push Jane up against this tree trunk and pash these memories of Evil Lauren right out of her head.

She balled her hands into fists. *Nope. Push the horniness down. WAY down. Nope, need to go lower than that! To the feet!*

Jane's frown was gone, and the cloud had passed.

I ditched that therapist anyway. Too many bird metaphors. "That's really shitty. I'm sorry that happened to you. Is there anything I can do, or not do, to accommodate your ASD?"

Jane shook her head. "You're easy to talk to. There's nothing you need to change."

Oof! The horniness rushed back through her in a big way. She turned her head away to hide a wince. "All right, so you've done the Walk of Fame," Amber said. "How about Venice Beach?"

Jane shook her head. "No, I haven't been there."

Amber bounced on the balls of her feet and clapped her hands. "Oo, good. It's quintessential LA. I'll take you. Are you free tomorrow?"

Jane's eyes fixed past her again, but only for a moment. She nodded.

"Yes? Yes! What time will I pick you up?"

They set off again through the park.

Amber was all glowy inside. She'd scored another date with Jane.

She was happy to respect Jane's pace, but today had confirmed something for Amber. She wanted Jane. The candlelit dinners, rose petals, the whole nine yards.

CHAPTER 8

"Careful!" said Jane as she grabbed Amber's arm, pulling her out of the path of a shirtless man tearing by them on an electric skateboard. She blinked, enjoying her hand on Amber's sleeve, being close, the vague hint of warm skin underneath.

Jane dropped the arm like it was a tree branch on fire.

Venice Beach had turned on a glorious day—crisp, cool and fresh. The waves crashed beyond the stretch of white sand as Jane and Amber continued along the boardwalk.

Being with Amber was easy, more fun that she could have imagined. She had stuck to her resolution to not overthink it and go with the flow. At least as much as she was capable of going with the flow.

Anxiety had crept in when Amber touched her wrist in the park the day before. It had sent a jolt through her.

Immediately her brain had sounded an alarm, along with a flashing sign. *Danger!*

On top of the physical effect Amber had on her, Jane found herself telling her things—secrets tumbling out of her mouth as if she had no control. She wasn't ashamed of her autism; in fact, since her diagnosis, her life had become easier in many ways. She knew why some things were harder for her than they seemed to be for other people and had discovered ways to manage.

But Lauren's jibes about her inadequacies were another matter. Jane had pushed them down a long way—it had taken many sessions for a skilled therapist to get anywhere near them.

Amber was enjoying charming her; Jane could see that. But the touch of her skin had woken something up in Jane, and she felt so comfortable with her. Talking to her, sharing things with her. Jane was anxious about how much she would give of herself just to make Amber smile.

Would Amber take her whimsical adventure even further and stir feelings up in Jane, just because she could?

Jane had seen no evidence that this was the case, but she didn't know her well enough to be certain. She couldn't shake the feeling that she was a naïve regular person who had stumbled into a game played by slick Hollywood types.

Sure, Mr Hairdo (who she now knew was named Teddy) and Amber didn't seem like cold, manipulative pretenders. They were perfectly nice, especially Amber.

But Jane didn't see a viable alternative theory to explain what was happening. Not even in her maddest daydreams could she imagine that Amber was attracted to her. She probably went to parties with Britney Spears and Kim Cattrall, and other people that had been in the movie *Crossroads*. Jane couldn't compete with that kind of glamour.

"You low-key just saved my life!" said Amber.

"Oh, er, don't mention it. People really tear through here, don't they?"

"Always. And it's way more crowded than this in summer. They shut this section down to film that scene in the *Barbie* movie, and there were hundreds if not thousands of people crowded around the barricades trying to see what was going on."

Jane looked around. "I remember that scene. Barbie and Ken are dressed as rodeo people."

Amber giggled. "Oh, so you do participate in popular culture. You saw *Barbie*?"

Jane smiled.

Amber was teasing her again.

It made her chest thrum. "I keep my finger on the pulse. *Barbie* actually has some quite interesting sociological ideas. It's ultimately a study of reflexivity. Barbie is forced to examine the assumptions that form the basis of her existence. The film asks the audience to think critically about power structures, which I'm trying to have my students do. I've shown some scenes in lectures."

The sea breeze picked up. Amber pulled her jacket tight across her chest.

Jane's arm twitched with an urge to wrap Amber up and hold her close. She shoved her hands into her pockets.

"It's so interesting how everything can have different meanings," said Amber. "It made me think about how Barbie's life is one big performance for the people around her." She shrugged and shook her head, then looked out at the sea.

Jane watched the distant waves for a few moments. "You know what other movie is very layered?" she asked.

Amber drew her gaze back to Jane and shook her head again.

"*Crossroads.*"

A warmth flooded through Jane as Amber grinned.

Jane nodded with mock earnestness. "Oh yes. Talk about feminist sociology? Anything you can't learn from Britney's physical and emotional journey in *Crossroads* is not worth knowing."

She was rewarded with a laugh and glowed with triumph.

They walked in silence for a while.

Jane wanted to lean into Amber's space, to have their arms in their thick jackets brush against each other, or even link together, to further blend their respective spaces into one. But she held herself upright and kept herself to herself. "Did you always want to be a singer?" she asked. "Sorry, you've probably answered that a hundred times. Sara probably knows the response."

"No, it's fine. I don't remember ever wanting to be anything else. When I was a kid, the times in between when I could be singing and dancing on stage seemed to totally drag by, then the performances themselves were a riot of fun and technicolour. I felt like my truest self on stage."

"Do you still?"

Amber puffed her cheeks out. "Now, that's a very good question." She closed her eyes for just a moment, then sucked a breath in through her teeth and glanced up at Jane. "I still love it, performing. But adult me has a lot of ways I get that happiness. I've learned balance. I was pushed a lot when I was younger, so my self-worth was tied up with 'success' as a singer. I've had to go back to basics and learn what I want, separate to what I was taught to want.

"Time in nature, dinner with friends, all that stuff. My truest self doesn't have a fixed address. She might live in the in-between areas."

Jane frowned, troubled. She wanted to express sympathy that Amber had been forced to strive like that. *Nope, too tricky. I'll muck it up for sure.* "I think I understand. Identity is a funny thing at the best of times. I just re-read a fascinating book from about five years ago about queer sociology and how the first bit of data most researchers collect ask is 'Are you male or female?' Queer theory now dictates that you start somewhere else, but a lot of people are frightened of what that means.

"To me it's incredibly exciting, to be able to gather, record, and understand the queer experience. Otherwise, these people get left out when policymakers are deciding what to do next."

She clamped her lips shut. *You're doing it again.* Too loud, too fast, too animated. She scanned Amber's face for signs that the enthusiasm she held for her own favourite topic was too over the top.

But Amber's eyes met hers, and she nodded with keen interest. "Sounds fascinating. I'd love to read it."

"Absolutely. It's called *Other, Please Specify.*" She was about to say it was dense, with detail on sociological research methodology, but clapped her mouth shut again. She didn't want Amber to think she was underestimating her. She had learned early on in her teaching career that people didn't need to wear tweed suits and have thick glasses to be smart. "I'll have to lend it to you sometime."

"Did you always want to be an associate professor of sociology and anthropology?"

"Yes," Jane said with no hesitation. "I always had questions. Question after question. I remember blowing out the candles of my birthday cake—I think I was seven—and wishing that I could ask all the questions I wanted without anyone getting tired of it. That seemed like a dream come true to me."

Amber hugged her arms across her chest. "Who gets scared?"

"Pardon?"

"You said people get scared of new thinking on queer research, um, thingy, you know, methods. Who does?"

"Oh, a lot of the people I work with, to be honest. It can be incredibly frustrating." Jane stepped away from Amber to avoid a rollerblader dashing past in the opposite direction wearing nothing but a triangle bikini (and blades, of course).

They moved back together, shoulder to shoulder, once the blader had passed in between them, like a river around a rock.

"Some decision-makers are obsessed with increasing the uni's standing and reputation internationally. Which is all well and good, except that it affects the research projects they'll allow and the curriculum. It makes them conservative. If anything is seen as too 'niche' for the international academic community, it's shot down."

Amber chuckled and shook her head.

Jane smiled too. "What?" She blinked, surprised by the absence of the spike of anxiety she usually felt when people laughed and she didn't know why. If she counted the number of people she felt that comfortable with, she could probably do it on her fingers. *And this woman is a stranger.* Again, the anxiety spike didn't happen. She quit trying to conjure it up.

"Nothing, just, it's funny how similar we are. I feel exactly the same about the entertainment industry sometimes. I felt for many years like they were always telling me no whenever I tried to do anything differently."

Jane's chest glowed warm. *Exactly the same.* She grinned. It was amusing, the two of them walking along—Jane tall and awkward, and Amber...beautiful. Moving with grace and ease. People glanced at her, and their gazes lingered because looking at her was a feel-good activity. "I'll have more autonomy when I'm associate professor."

"That's good. I'll have more autonomy when I'm Taylor Swift," Amber replied, laughing. "I'm sure my big break is just around the corner."

Jane laughed along with her, probably more than the joke warranted. Joy bubbled up like a wellspring as they walked along together. Goodwill emanated out of her towards everyone on the boardwalk today. She locked laughing eyes with a tanned leathery man with a grey beard and the words *Live Free* tattooed across his bare stomach.

He grinned back, revealing that he only had two teeth in his whole head, and gave her a thumbs up.

Jane giggled again as they walked by. The tattoo probably referenced the desire to bear a gun without a background check or not be restricted to having only one wife, but in that moment, the slogan struck a chord with her. Maybe she could *live free* from the past and from everything that had been holding her back. "I really like it here," she said. "Thank you for bringing me."

"Oh, I'm so glad. Maybe you could start hanging out here all the time. Join a blading gang with Bikini Woman. And I saw you vibing with Tanned Santa back there."

"Who knew my people were here waiting for me for the last thirty-nine years?"

"It looks like your old, bearded mate has been here waiting for you for twice that long."

They chuckled some more, then both sighed at the same time as the laughter ebbed away.

The sun grew large and orange as it sank towards the sea. Jane's life existed over on the other side of that ocean. It wasn't bathed in a golden glow like she was at that moment, though, strolling along with a near stranger. Had it ever been? A streak of grey shot through the afternoon at the thought.

She rolled her shoulders to shake off her negativity. *Live free. You can do anything you want.* She snuck a glance at Amber in the golden light.

CHAPTER 9

"The snow is fire, Jane."

"Oh?"

"You know what I mean. It's epic."

"Good, then?"

Sara scoffed on the other end of the video call. "Yes, good. You should come up and ski with us."

"You know I would love to, but who would look after Selena Gomez?"

The brown, grey and white moggie with black stripes raised her head, chirped, and slinked across the couch and onto Jane's lap.

"Aw, you remembered her full name. Is she keeping you company? I feel bad we left so soon after Christmas. Are you lonely?"

Selena purred and rubbed the side of her face against Jane's hand. "Um, no. Of course I miss you and your mum and dad. But I've been keeping myself occupied."

"Look, that's great. Selena's a great listener, and I'm always here if you need a chat. Well, Dad won't let me take my phone on the slopes after last year when I took that tumble with my brand new iPhone 13 in my ski suit. Luckily, the smashed screen ripped my pants and not my leg! Anyway, when I'm not on my board, I'm at your disposal."

"Thank you." Jane fought to keep her face neutral. She couldn't blame Sara—if it weren't for Amber, she would have probably only spoken to her far-off family and Selena Gomez in the past three days.

As it was, she had spoken about herself, her worldview, and her struggles, dreams and ambitions so much that her insides were an empty bucket. In a good way, though.

Her lips twitched, and she shook her head. New and unusual feelings had been forming as multicoloured bubbles within her since her first meet-up with Amber. Some of them difficult to describe.

"What, what is it?" Sara asked.

Uh-oh. She must have caught Jane's look.

The doorbell ding-donged through the house.

Phew! "I better go see who that is," Jane said, padding down the stairs in her socks, phone camera still pointed towards her. "Hello, may I help you?" she asked the top of the head in the video image on the little screen next to the front door.

The top of the head moved upwards, revealing a face. Amber's face.

"Hi. Jane? I—"

"Whoa!" Jane unpressed the gate intercom button, so Amber finished the sentence she was saying as a mini black-and-white mime on the screen.

"Who is it?" asked Sara.

"Uhhhhh, charity collector. Yes, that's it. One of those organisations... bringing in rescue dogs from Ecuador."

Jane's eyes were fixed on the intercom screen. Amber took a step back and looked back and forth down the street, as if considering leaving.

No! Jane held her phone to her face and spoke quickly. "I'd better get this, Sara. Much love to you and your parents. Stay safe out on those slopes. Bye, now."

"OK, bye. Talk soon. Wait, how did the collector know your name?" Sara's forehead was furrowed.

"Oh, well, I must have signed up as a donor at some stage. These groups are so aggressive with their fundraising these days. You should write to your city councillor. Bye, now."

Amber had disappeared from the screen.

Shit!

"See ya, Jane. Wait, you know Mum and Dad won't want a dog at the house. Selena would—"

Jane ended the call. Sending a silent apology to her niece, she opened the front door and sprinted down the garden path. A few steps before the gate, her anxiety spiked at the thought that Amber might have left. "Amber!" she called out. She reached the tall gate in the massive front fence, wrenched the handle, and pulled.

Amber stood right in front of her.

"Amber! I'm glad you didn't leave. Sorry, I didn't recognise you at first in the video. With your hair pulled back."

Amber pressed her lips together, eyes twinkling. She looked Jane up and down. "You've got your socks wet."

Jane froze as if a prison tower searchlight had caught her trying to break out. She took a mental inventory of how she looked: old boxer shorts, gym socks, hair not touched since she rolled out of bed, a University of Queensland footy team hoodie a student had given her as a gift. *Shit.* And, of course, it never rained in LA in winter except the night before, leaving grimy puddles all over the ground.

Amber's lips quivered, then she grinned.

Jane smiled in return. She relaxed like an ice statue thawing. *Who cares if she sees me unpolished?* It was kind of freeing. "Won't you come in?"

"Don't mind if I do."

As Jane led her up the path, a thought struck her. *What is she doing here?* A buzz started up in her chest. Unexpected things had never been her favourite, but being put on unexpected footing by Amber was exciting. And fun.

In the high-ceilinged entrance hall, Jane shut the door behind Amber and took a step back. There was a beat of silence.

Amber cleared her throat. "I hope you don't mind. I was in the area, and I thought I'd pop in and see if I could borrow that book you mentioned."

Jane's forehead furrowed. She must have looked just as Sara had when she spun that Ecuadorian rescue dog story. It didn't quite add up. Couldn't she have texted?

Jane blinked. *Look, she's here. That's not a bad thing. Now, where are your manners?* "Yes, of course. *Other, please specify—Queer Methods in Sociology.* I think it's here in the living room. Come this way." She was minutely aware of Amber walking close behind her. At the entrance to the living room, she stopped. "Hold on."

Amber was so close behind her, she could hear her breathing in the big, empty house.

Jane bent one knee then the other, removed her mucky socks, and dropped them on the tiles. "The carpet in here's new," she said. She didn't turn around to face Amber. She wasn't quite sure why not.

Selena ran in and snaked back and forth between Jane's bare calves.

"Oh, precious!" Amber said, crouching down and holding out a hand.

The cat pressed the top of her head against Amber's palm so hard that her front paws left the ground. Her purrs echoed in the tiled room.

"Her name's Selena Gomez," Jane said, thanking the cat inwardly for breaking the tension.

"Oh, how hilarious! Does she meow in English and Spanish?"

Jane frowned. "Pardon me?"

"Oh." She jumped up and Selena weaved back and forth, bashing her forehead against Amber. "You know, she records albums in both languages."

"Uhhhhhh." *I've completely lost the thread here.*

"Wait, you have no idea who Selena Gomez is, do you? The person, I mean."

Jane nodded slowly. "You know, I never thought to ask. Sara named her, and whenever I question anything Sara does, I usually end up more befuddled after the explanation."

Amber snorted with laughter, then rested her fingertips against her top lip. "Sorry. I shouldn't come into your house unannounced and laugh at you."

Jane fought to keep her expression neutral. Amber thought Jane was funny. Jane waited for the unease that usually pricked at her when people laughed at her, but it didn't come. Rather, Amber's smile made Jane tingle behind her ears.

"I'm kind of offended the cat's not named after me."

Jane smiled and led the way into the living room. "Don't worry, there are probably better namesakes out there that you have more in common with. Unless you like rolling around in the sun and licking yourself." Her shoulders stiffened, and she stopped walking. The heat rushed to her face, and she wheeled around to face Amber. "Sorry, I... That was a strange thing to say."

Amber had the fingertips of both hands pressed to her mouth, and her eyes were wide.

Oh, no, no, no! I've made it weird.

Amber made a choking noise, then a laugh escaped, shaking her shoulders. She waved her hands. "No! That was a great thing to say. A-plus."

Jane pinched the bridge of her nose and smiled as her panic dissipated slightly but didn't go away. "Here." She spotted the book in the middle of a pile on the coffee table and scooped it up.

"Oh, great. Thanks. Gosh, this is a lovely room." Amber sighed as she got her breath back.

"Yeah, Barbara and Bill designed the house and had it built a couple of years ago. This room's my favourite. I love a comfy armchair to read in."

"This outlook is divine!" said Amber, moving to the full-length window with a view of the enclosed back garden. The sunlight streamed in. She took off her jacket and draped it over the back of a chair, walking as if transfixed by the greenery outside.

Jane rounded the couch on the other side and approached the window. She wanted to point out her favourite desert willow tree.

She stopped short, the description of the tree's autumn flowers dying on her lips.

The winter sun streamed in through the window. It illuminated Amber's face with gold, bringing into focus the tiny lines running softly across her face.

Jane hadn't seen them before—they must have been hidden under a layer of expert make-up.

A quiet smile played across Amber's mouth as she ran her eyes over the colours and textures of the garden.

The top of Jane's chest ached. Her hand twitched. She wanted to run her fingertips across Amber's face—follow the map of fine lines that were evidence of countless smiles, laughs, and tears. She wanted to touch her lips. Taste them. She clutched tight to the book in her hand, worried it might slip through her fingers.

What the dickens is happening? She had acknowledged to herself many times over the past couple of days that Amber was beautiful, mesmerising an entire audience at the concert. Fans queued up for hours to lay eyes on her, and strangers turned their heads to look at her as she walked by them on the street.

But this? Jane exhaled a shuddering breath as quietly as she could. *I need to get a handle on myself!* It wasn't like Amber had gone to any trouble. She was much more dressed down than usual.

From her side-on standpoint, she moved her eyes away from Amber's glorious face to her yellow T-shirt. She hoped it would give her back some control over her body.

The T-shirt was soft and well-worn, comfortable, clinging in all the right places.

Oh dear.

Hot desire coursed through Jane. She tried to inhale but couldn't quite manage it. Her body was too busy fighting the urge to flatten her palms across Amber's belly and slide the soft fabric up to reveal the warm skin beneath.

What noise would Amber make if Jane pressed her mouth to the skin just above her jeans?

Jane needed air. She breathed in quickly, making a sound like a strangled gasp, then huffed out again with a splutter-cough. Her toes curled into the thick merino carpet.

Amber turned towards her, mouth quirking up on one side. "Hah! Sorry. I got a bit lost in the niceness that is your sister's garden. Oh, great, here's the book." She walked the few steps to where Jane was standing. Glancing up at her face, her eyes narrowed for a second.

Jane might not have noticed, if her entire consciousness hadn't been fixated on the woman in front of her.

As it was, the brief deepening of the laugh lines around Amber's eyes was as obvious as a massive billboard on the Sunset Strip.

Amber took the book in her hand, although Jane wasn't offering it to her as such.

More like it was dangling from Jane's hand as she stood frozen, longing and embarrassment intermingling in her body.

Jane didn't let go of the book.

Amber ran her other hand across the hardcover and rested the tips of her fingers against Jane's clammy hand. Her gaze moved from their hands to Jane's face.

Amber's gaze held questions.

What do you see? What do you feel? It was like Jane heard the words in her head. She blinked.

Amber looked back down at the dry and dense sociology book.

Jane didn't let go.

Amber nodded, as if Jane had given some kind of response. "Jane?"

"Yah." She winced. She was reduced to uttering inarticulate sounds.

Amber took the book in both hands, holding it against her stomach.

Jane dropped her hands.

"Will you come to a party with me tomorrow night?" Amber asked.

Yah!

"To be clear, I'm asking you as my plus-one. My date. Is that OK? It's at a friend's house in the Hills. Well, he's not really a friend, just a guy at the label, but he's famous for his parties. They're usually fun."

"Yes," said Jane. Her heart hammered, making every part of her body thrum. *A date!* That meant Amber liked her too. The realisation, so simple, an impossible daydream a high-schooler might have, opened like a delicate flower in her mind, glowing radiant.

Amber bounced on the spot once and clapped her hands. "Good! That's good."

"There's not going to be a red carpet or anything, is there?" asked Jane, her cheeks hurting from smiling.

Amber laughed. "No, nothing like that. There'll be some food, a bar by the pool. It's just like any normal party you'd go to, really."

"I'm not so sure about that. The last party I went to was to celebrate a colleague receiving a sabbatical fellowship. He read to us from a book of Winston Churchill's witticisms for a large chunk of the evening."

Amber laughed.

Jane thrilled at what the laughter did to Amber's body—her face moving involuntarily with a bubbling joy that came from deep within. Causing this reaction in her gave Jane a high. She could imagine getting hooked on this feeling, which was part physical longing and part giddy anticipation.

Tomorrow night. It pulsed with possibilities. Maybe Amber would laugh and Jane would press her lips to her soft neck.

"Great, well. Tomorrow night, then. I'll text you the info." Amber twitched her head in the direction of the door but made no other motion to leave.

"Fantastic! Yes. Shoot that info through. I'll need all the, uh, deets." Jane winced.

"Hah! Yep, that you will." Amber flicked a thumbs up, then held the book up with both hands as if remembering she had a prop. "Thanks so much for the book. I can't wait to read it."

"Ohhh, yes. Such an important topic. You're welcome."

Amber still made no move to leave.

Was she moving towards Jane, shifting her weight to the balls of her feet?

No. *Phew!* If Amber had given her a hug or a peck on the cheek goodbye, Jane may have exploded – the gruesome damage done to her sister's mid-century modern interior inexcusable.

Jane's awareness of the empty house whirled outwards. They were surrounded by empty bedrooms, sofas–hell, even a stylish choice of unoccupied tabletops. Alone together. Amber had asked her out for real. Would it be so bad if she strode through the space between them and kissed her, as her body was crying out for her to do?

"Tomorrow night, then," Amber repeated.

"Yes, yeah. Let me walk you out." She gestured, letting Amber turn and walk ahead of her. She puffed out a breath and shook her shoulders, maintaining a few steps' distance.

This was the way it should be. Amber wanted a proper date, maybe as a demonstration of serious intent. Jane would respect her wishes. Appearances could be deceiving—maybe Amber was kind of old-fashioned in that way. Like people who wanted suitors to ask for their father's permission before proposing marriage. Did Amber's dad live in Australia or the US?

Amber spoke, but Jane cleared her throat loudly and missed it. *Pull yourself together!* "I beg your pardon?"

"See you tomorrow," Amber said.

"Yah! Uh, yes. Tomorrow it is."

Amber gave a long nod, kind of an awkward half bow, then pushed open the front door and was gone.

As it clicked shut behind her, Jane slumped against the wall, sliding down until she was sitting on the floor with her knees up.

Tomorrow night. Not long to wait. Tomorrow was Tuesday. Tuesday, the thirty-first of December.

Her stomach dipped. *New Year's Eve.* She was going to a New Year's Eve event thrown by some Hollywood man famous for his parties.

Amber's invitation took on a new weight—a heaviness of expectation.

Jane rested the back of her head against the cool wall. The pent-up pressure forced a bark of laughter out of her, followed by another and another. The laughter echoed off the double-height ceiling and through the empty house.

CHAPTER 10

Jane held on for dear life as the Uber sped around the hairpin turns of the Hollywood Hills. Barbara and Bill had taken her for a drive up there to look at mansions and see the sunset on a previous visit. That time, she had felt carsick, and tonight was worse.

"Could you slow down a little, please?" she asked.

"Yeah, yeah. No problem. I know these roads like the back of my hand, though. I'm up here most days. Last week, I dropped Kaley Cuoco off at her home. Nice place. I've had others too. Timothee Chalamet, Faye Dunaway, and Mariska Hargitay!" He looked sideways at Jane.

Oh great. My last moments on earth are going to be spent having gibberish words spoken at me as I careen off a cliff. "Oh. Wow," she said, praying that would be enough to get his eyes back onto the narrow road.

She regretted not driving herself. She had been anxious about navigating the treacherous hills, but at least she would have maintained a sensible speed.

"Where ya headed? Fancy party?"

Jane looked down at her deep-maroon suit and nice shoes. She had bought the outfit to go to Sara's high school graduation, and it always made her feel confident. She hoped it would cut it at this Hollywood event.

"Yes. A New Year's celebration. Oop, here we are."

He let out a low whistle. "Geeeee whiz, swanky place. Someone famous own this place?"

"I'm not sure. Thank you for driving me."

"Anyone famous going to be here?" he asked as Jane shut the door.

She waved at him, and he drove off. She looked up at the high concrete fence—with a stunning mansion precariously cantilevered into the cliff face above it, lit from outside and within—and let out a low whistle of her own.

Her stomach wobbled around like it was full of unset jelly. She wanted to dive back into the safety of her Uber, which, a minute ago, had felt like a deathtrap. The house was too fancy. She didn't belong in a place like this, with the type of people that hung around in a place like this!

Amber *fit* in a place like this. It made sense for an invitation to this party to be extended to Amber. She shone, like the impossible house towering above Jane.

"Excuse me, ma'am."

Jane wheeled around. A tall, broad man in a dark suit standing next to the metal gate beckoned her over. He was wearing sunglasses even though the sun had set a couple of hours before.

"Yes?" said Jane.

"I'm sorry, but if you're not on the list, you need to vacate the premises." He motioned with an iPad he was holding.

"Oh, of course," said Jane. *What do you mean 'of course'? You've never been to a party with a beefy bouncer before! And what city by-laws allow private residents to not allow other private residents to stand for a few moments on the public footpath in front of their house? Everyone in this city thinks they own the world!*

Jane was about to ask the man about the by-laws, but he cleared his throat and gestured with the device once more.

"My name is Jane Miles?" It came out like a question, like she was unsure of her own identity.

"Thank you, ma'am. Enjoy your evening. And Happy New Year." He opened the gate and half bowed at her as she walked through.

"Um, yes. Same to you," said Jane, a little surprised at being let in. Amber had not mentioned anything about a list in the texts they had exchanged.

Jane ascended a steep, curving driveway. The property was amazing, but a big part of her wanted to turn tail and abandon this crazy endeavour. During the day, up until she got in that getaway car disguised as an Uber, she had been looking forward to seeing Amber again. She had enjoyed texting back and forth. Her phone was usually pretty quiet, except sometimes when Sara had read a new book or watched a new sci-fi show she wanted to tell Jane about. Then her phone would ping all day.

But it hit different when her phone lit up with a text from a beautiful woman. A woman who took Jane's breath away simply by looking out a window at plants. Every text was a little offering, an indication that Amber was thinking about her, looking forward to seeing her at the party.

Jane's emotions still hadn't caught up to what was happening. She was all swept up and turned about. Amber had said yesterday that this was a date. A proper date to a New Years' party. Amber had been upfront and clear—no games or "maybes" or ambiguity. Jane had liked it. A lot.

There was still this little sliver of doubt, though. Amber was a performer, a showwoman. The last two days since she had met Amber had been the most exciting of her life. Well, maybe not as exciting as landing a big research grant or tallying up comprehensive datasets to find something truly unexpected or fascinating. But this little rendezvous had been the most glamourous and out-of-the-ordinary thing to ever happen to her. Maybe Amber enjoyed blowing the minds of ordinary, humdrum people and would get bored with Jane once the thrill had worn off.

Jane was used to basing her conclusions on evidence, and everything she had seen about Amber so far pointed to the fact that she was a nice, honest, funny person. Not someone who used people for little adventures and cast them aside.

One mystery remained, though: What did she see in Jane?

Jane shook her head. These types of questions, these trains of thought, were things she needed to watch out for. But it was hard, given how her last relationship had turned out.

She finally reached the top of the drive. There was a huge garage under the house with all its doors open, expensive-looking cars inside it lit up as if in a showroom. People must drive right up, she figured, although the walk was excellent cardio. To her right was a deck with a rectangular pool with people milling around it. Music played, and strings of lights festooned the area.

About a dozen people in chic clothes chatted in clumps. A quick scan told her that none of them were Amber. She took a deep breath and stepped from the relative darkness of the driveway into the lights of the deck. Her nervousness evaporated, and she stood stock-still as she took in the view beyond the pool's edge. The lights of LA lay out before her like a sparkling carpet. It was breathtaking.

Jane could have looked at the view all night, but she rolled back her shoulders and tore her gaze away. It was bad manners to stand silently by yourself at parties, whether they were morning teas in the campus staff room because someone was off to have a baby, or fancy mansion soirees like this one. She wandered further away from the safety and privacy of the driveway, threading her way between pairs or groups of three partygoers talking and laughing. Jane spotted someone serving drinks from behind a high bar with a white tablecloth. She veered that way.

"Hello, what can I get you?" the server asked with a smile. She was young, not much older than Jane's bachelor's students, and had a completely shaved head.

"Oh, um, a beer, please."

"Pilsener, helles or IPA?"

"Uhhhh, the second one? Thank you."

"You betcha. One helles coming right up." She put a frosty bottle on the bar.

Jane reached for it.

"Woop, sorry there, ma'am. Let me open that up for you. Unless you're going to do it with your teeth."

Jane winced. *Obvious!*

The server wrenched the top off with a flourish. "There you are. Enjoy."

"Thank you." Jane took the drink.

There was a pause.

"Should I pay you for it?"

"Oh! Nooooo." Now it was the server's turn to wince. "Open bar for guests." She glanced sideways at a large jar on the bar next to her. "But you are more than welcome to tip, if you want? All us caterers will split the kitty at the end."

Jane winced some more.

Jane's anxiety was mirrored in the server's expression, and they stood frozen for a moment.

Jane sucked air through her teeth. "I'm so sorry. We don't do the small bills thing where I'm from. I know I've got to get accustomed to it, but I haven't yet. But my friend has lived here longer, and she'll have some for sure. Can I write you an IOU?" As soon as the words left her lips she knew they were daft. "We don't tip in Australia. We try to pay people a living wage instead. Oh, pardon me, that was a very rude thing to say. I..." Jane trailed off, her face burning.

The server pressed her lips together but could not suppress her chuckle.

Jane scoffed at herself. "I'm sorry. I'm not used to being at parties like this."

"Hey, don't sweat it." She leaned towards Jane. "Listen, I've catered dozens of parties just like this. They're no different from teenage basement parties, or parties my improv class throws in dingy bars. Nobody's having as much fun as they're pretending to have, and nobody wants to be the one standing alone by the snack table. You got this."

Jane exhaled. "Thank you." She lifted her bottle to the server as she walked away.

A young man walked up to her. "Hello," he said. "I'm Archer. I'm an actor."

"Hi Archer. I'm Jane."

"I've just booked a role with a three-episode arc on a newly commissioned sitcom with Kaley Cuoco."

Jane narrowed her eyes. That name was vaguely familiar.

"What do you do?" asked Archer.

"I teach sociology and anthropology."

"Ohhhhhh." Archer's brow furrowed, and he cocked his head. "Do you consult on screenplays or scripts?"

"No."

"Sociology? Is that something to do with TikTok optimisation?"

Jane raised her eyebrows. This conversation was veering right off any track she was familiar with. "No."

Archer ran his fingers through his blonde, tousled hair. Then he pointed his finger in Jane's face. "Wait! Social-lo-logists. They have them on reality dating shows. You know, diagnosing the heck out of all the contestants. Are you on *Bachelor in Paradise UK*?"

Jane shook her head. "No. I'm a senior lecturer at the University of Queensland."

Archer frowned. "Cool. Cool. Well, it was great to meet you, Jamie-Lee." He turned his back and walked off.

Jane shrugged as she was left alone holding her bottle of beer. She was usually good with young people. Her students were always giving the uni feedback that she was an engaging teacher. But these last two back-to-back interactions, especially the last one, had left her bewildered. Amber seemed normal, but she must speak a totally different language and live a life Jane couldn't even imagine to be able to navigate social situations like this all the time.

She looked around, trying not to cringe at what her next conversation might bring.

Past the poolside hedges, back in the driveway, a man in a floral shirt had jumped out of the driver's seat and was running around to open the passenger door.

Jane squinted. *Mr Hairdo!* That meant...

Amber emerged from the car. Bewilderment and unease gave way to a thrumming in Jane's chest. Mr Hairdo said something, and Amber shook her head. He headed back around the car and got in.

Amber moved towards the party. Her face lit up into a smile when she saw Jane.

She was wearing a deep-pink shiny dress with a short skirt and a long blue fur coat that came down to her knees. Her hair was big and fancy again.

Jane smiled back. A thud of anticipation beat through her, like it hadn't in many years. She remembered being young and newly out and hitting up the gay pub at the top of Spring Hill in Brisbane. The thrilling potential for closeness and touch. Losing all control in the search for pleasure and release.

Jane cleared her throat. *Whoa!* One flash of nice legs in a short dress and she was all steamed up like a Korean bathhouse.

Amber walked towards her. The other party guests faded into the background. Even the view of the city through the frameless glass fencing was garbage compared to her.

"Hi," Jane said.

"Hi yourself."

A pause. Should Jane hug her? The moment passed.

"It's faux," said Amber.

"Pardon me?"

Amber laughed. "The jacket. It's not real fur."

"Oh, yeah, I figured. Unless you had your assistant go out a poach you the last royal blue polar bear left in the wild."

"I'm not looking to get cancelled—this year at least."

"Well, you've almost made it through."

They both chuckled.

"I'm so sorry I was late," said Amber. "I wanted to get here first, but my hair lady was late. Were you OK?"

"Yes. Definitely. I've been making friends. Rubbing shoulders. In fact, I think I may have landed a three-episode arc in a newly commissioned television sitcom."

Amber raised her eyebrows. "Well, well, well. Fame and fortune await."

"That reminds me. I hate to ask, but can I borrow some money? I didn't have anything to put in the bartender's jar."

She grinned. "You gotta carry around those small bills, Jane. Your Aussie accent and confusion about tipping will only get you so far. Do you know what I have in this bag?"

Jane looked at the tiny, slim clutch she held up. "Half a Vegemite sandwich with the crusts cut off?"

"Close. My phone, that I have to take out of the case to even fit it in here, and a small wad of one- and five-dollar bills. Come on, let's uncancel you in the eyes of the catering staff."

They approached the bar.

"Me again," said Jane.

"Oh, hi. You here to open more beer bottles with your teeth?" asked the bartender.

Jane shoved one of Amber's bills into the jar and scrunched it down. "I was able to borrow some money, so here's the tip I owe you and your friends."

The bartender inclined her head and gestured doffing an imaginary hat. "Thank you kindly. But don't lose any sleep over us. We'll split the leftover food at the end of the night. Nobody eats anything at these industry parties. I'll start out the year with four days' worth of lobster and beluga caviar. Can I get you another drink? Same again?"

"Oh, well, yes, please. But..."

Amber put her hand on Jane's arm. "I'll spring you another tip, don't worry. And I'll have one of what Jane's having please."

"Thanks," said Jane. "I promise I'll pay you back."

Amber took her drink. "Don't stress. I'm certain I can think of a way for you to make it up to me." She addressed the bartender with a smile. "Thank you."

Jane's face burned as a thrill shot down her body. It was suddenly difficult to breathe. She cleared her throat and grabbed her drink.

The bartender raised her eyebrows and grinned, giving Jane a slow nod and thumbs up as Jane turned to follow Amber back into the growing crowd.

CHAPTER 11

"And the screenplay was written by Michelle Pfeiffer's dogwalker!"

Jane glanced sideways at Amber, who grimaced for a split second then plastered a shining smile back onto her face. They were stuck in a small circle being yelled at by a loud, bald man. His coherence was decreasing as his champagne intake went up. The party was getting louder and looser.

Jane and Amber stood close together. Jane could feel the heat from Amber's skin through her sleeve.

"Oh, that reminds me, Amber, baby, I gotta introduce you to that booker from Chicago. Sorry, I gotta steal this little girl away for a moment." He put his arm around Amber and steered her away.

Jane almost reached out and held her back. She had the urge to give the loud guy a little shove, but she also didn't want to touch him.

Amber looked back over the top of his big arm and snorted when she caught sight of Jane's face. *Sorry,* she mouthed.

Jane shook her shoulders and tried to make her expression neutral. She gave Amber a thumbs up.

The little circle dispersed as soon as the nonsense-shouting man had gone. Jane looked around her. She didn't want to stand there alone with her feelings. She felt a kind of dull rage at the universe that Amber was not standing there next to her. It was worrying.

Her decision-making over the past couple of days had started from a place of curiosity, of wanting to shake her life up a bit and see where this strange adventure would take her. But Amber was amazing, and Jane calculated that the depth of her desire was out of proportion with how much time they had spent together, how many conversations they had had.

The attraction was chemical, and unpredictable. She needed to not get lost in it.

A man nearby wearing a bottle-green suit and sandals, despite the night-time chill, had just finished a call and was putting his phone away.

Jane approached him. "Hello," she said.

"Hi," he said, flicking his gaze just past Jane's head, as if looking for someone to come and rescue him.

She was not going to be discouraged. "I'm Jane."

The young man mumbled something back. The music had gotten progressively louder as the party had worn on.

Jane leaned in closer and noticed he appeared to be wearing a thick layer of foundation concealer. "What was that, sorry? Tom?"

His eyes darted more desperately. "No, um, sorry, I think I see my assistant. Bye." And he was off.

Jane swung around to watch him go.

He glanced back and walked faster when he met her eyes.

"What a strange young man," Jane said to herself.

A hand pressed into the small of her back, and she looked down to see Amber. "Oh, thank God."

"Sorry for abandoning you. Were you OK?"

"Yes, sorry. I'm just glad you're not somebody else."

Amber smiled. "Well I'm very glad you're not somebody else too."

Warmth shot through Jane, radiating from where Amber was touching her.

"I saw you talking to Anton Brewer. Did you get a photo for Sara?"

"Who's Anton Brewer? That skinny nervous man just now? Do you know him?"

"I know *of* him. He's one of the hottest actors in Hollywood right now. Total A-list. He was in that arty movie where everyone spoke in tongues for the whole second act, and he's going to star in the new remake of *Herbie the Love Bug*. Wait, you mean to tell me you've never heard of him?"

Jane bit her bottom lip, not able to hide her smile. "I called him Tom, then he ran away."

Amber's shoulders started to shake as she laughed. Tears formed in the corners of her eyes. "Sorry," she gasped. "The guy throwing this party has been obsessed with getting Anton Brewer here. He's a massive get. And you..." she tried to catch her breath. "You called him Tom." She grasped hold of Jane's shoulders, laughing fit to burst.

Jane laughed too, enjoying Amber's uncontrollable glee, but also how tightly Amber was holding her.

Amber sighed. "Jane, this is honestly the most fun I've had at a party in as long as I can remember. I wish I could keep you around forever."

Jane's breath caught in her throat. She cast around for something to say, scared that the moment would pass and Amber would let her go. "I think a lot of these people are wondering what you're doing here with me. They probably think I'm your accountant."

Amber raised her face a little closer to Jane's, her chuckles subsiding to a soft smile. "I know these people better than you do. They're thinking, who's that amazingly attractive woman who has her shit so together, who isn't thrumming on a frequency of frenzied insecurity and desperation for approval. They all want to break off a piece of you and keep it for themselves." She moved closer, her body brushing against Jane's. "Plus, I have the same accountant as a few of the people here. He does a drag show every Thursday night at Lash in Mission Junction."

Jane smiled. Amber's life was a glamourous mystery, so different from her own. She was funny and interesting. Jane was intoxicated by her.

Amber ran her hand down Jane's arm and clasped her hand. "Come with me." She led her into the house through a massive open door.

Amber's heels clacked noisily on the marble floor of a giant living room. She moved swiftly, letting go of Jane's hand as they reached the top of the stairs.

Jane was chilled by her closeness with Amber being taken away so suddenly, but the low lights on the landing and the fact they were now alone started a fire low in her belly.

Amber opened a door. "There are probably cameras all through the garden, but not"—she dragged Jane through and closed the door behind her—"in the guest bedrooms."

The lights were off, but the room was lit through massive glass doors by the party lights below. The bass pounding with so much less volume than outside made Jane feel as if she'd fallen into water.

Amber pulled Jane towards her and wrapped her arms tight around her middle. "I want to kiss you. Can I kiss you?"

The thin veneer of control that Jane had kept in place the day before, and for the hours they had been at this party, shattered to a million tiny pieces.

Amber had her arms around her. Amber's belly was pressed to hers.

It was so *good* that Jane's blood roared in her ears.

"Yes," Jane whispered, not able to control her breath enough to speak any louder.

Amber pressed her mouth to Jane's, hard. Her tongue found Jane's, and desire throbbed through Jane's body with such force that she gasped.

Jane held the sides of Amber's face, her mouth open and her tongue pressing against Amber's again and again. The answering pressure from Amber and her soft moans made Jane desperate for more. She wanted Amber completely.

Amber pushed her against the wall and pulled her head down towards her own so she could kiss Jane's mouth more fully.

Jane grasped Amber's hips and pulled her close.

Amber pressed into Jane, who moved her hips against her body.

After one final purposeful sweep of her tongue, Amber looked down at where their bellies and hips met. Breathing hard, she pulled Jane's shirt loose from where it was tucked into her trousers.

Amber brushed her fingers like a whisper over Jane's bared belly.

Heat seared through Jane, a building desire that took her breath away. But her chest was also heavy with a tenderness. She ran her thumb down Amber's cheek and kissed her again.

Amber's breath caught as she kissed Jane back. Jane could feel every soft movement of Amber's mouth in every part of her body.

A series of distant bangs sounded in the distance. Then more and more.

Amber's mouth on hers curled into a smile.

Amber stepped sideways and snuggled herself into Jane's side, wrapping her arms around her. Together they watched the LA skyline explode in a multitude of colours.

Amber brushed her lips against Jane's jawline. "Happy New Year," she whispered.

CHAPTER 12

Jane's sister's house was six minutes closer than Amber's according to the Lyft app.

They bid a swift farewell to the other party guests. Amber gave a guy called Kade a peck on the cheek.

Jane swiped her phone screen to check on the status of their ride. *Goodbye Kade, goodbye Tom. Let's get out of here!*

The car took a while to arrive, but it worked out fine because it took a long time to walk down the steep cliff-face driveway.

Their driver had blue hair and kept up a steady stream of conversation. What did they do for work? What kind of accent is that? Any New Year's resolutions? She had been initially interested that Amber was a singer but became instantly bored when it turned out she didn't perform ska music.

Jane's heartbeat was pulsing in her throat.

Amber held her hand tight and was running her thumb along the sensitive skin at Jane's wrist.

She squirmed in her seat and craned her neck to look at the driver's phone in its holder by the windscreen.

Thirteen minutes!

Amber kept up a polite conversation with the driver. No, she had never met the band Reel Big Fish. Or Streetlight Manifesto.

Jane watched her while she spoke. The urge to throw herself across the back seat and press her entire body against every part of Amber's was so strong, it was frightening.

Amber shot her a sideways glance and waggled her eyebrows, holding Jane's hand tighter.

Jane cleared her throat. She was barely keeping it together.

Finally they arrived. Jane fumbled with the gate code on the tall concrete fence. She led Amber by the hand through her sister's small front garden and fumbled again with the keypad by the front door.

"Shit, sorry. It will be a situation if I don't disable the alarm," Jane said through gritted teeth.

Amber laughed and stroked Jane's arm. "Relax. I'm not going anywhere."

She exhaled loudly and keyed the code in successfully.

Jane switched on the light. Then she pulled Amber by the hand and wrapped her arms tightly around her.

Amber snaked her arms around Jane's middle and kissed her hard.

Jane returned the pressure, her body thrilling at every movement of Amber's tongue against hers.

"Where's your bedroom?" Amber asked. Her voice echoed in the empty house.

"Upstairs," said Jane.

"Lead on." Amber pushed her towards the stairs.

Jane stumbled in her hurry to get to the top.

On the landing, Amber grabbed her around the middle again and kissed her jawline from behind.

Jane gasped as heat coursed through her body. She spun around and pressed Amber gently against the wall.

Amber bit her bottom lip and whispered, "There's something I've been really wanting to do."

Jane raised her eyebrows.

Amber reached down and slid one of her shoes off, then the other, and kicked them towards the stairs. She groaned and threw her head back as her soles hit the carpet.

"Goodness, you're short," said Jane.

Amber laughed. "It takes eight-inch heels for people to be able to see me from behind shop counters."

"Whoops, where are my manners?" said Jane and slipped off her shoes and socks, kicking them after Amber's.

Amber looked down and wiggled her toes next to Jane's.

The tickle of skin on skin sent warm waves up through Jane's body.

Pressing her forehead against Jane's cheek, Amber breathed deeply. She ran her fingers along Jane's belt.

Jane held her breath, ran her hands along Amber's back and started undoing the zipper of her dress.

"God, yes," said Amber and undid Jane's belt and pants.

Jane took half a hop backwards and pulled her pants off as Amber pulled her dress from her shoulders and wiggled it down her hips.

Jane's breath caught as her eyes roamed over Amber's flat belly, the curve of her hips. Her eyes lingered on Amber's breasts, barely covered by a strapless bra.

Amber smiled as she slowly undid the bra and took it off, revealing small, perfect breasts.

Jane's breath came out as an uncontrolled pant. She met Amber's eyes, then flung her pants back over her shoulder, over the landing and down into the entrance hall.

Amber shouted with laughter and tossed her dress and bra after Jane's clothes.

She took hold of the sides of Jane's face and kissed her again.

Jane covered one of Amber's breasts with her hand, delighting in the warmth and softness.

That made Amber moan softly, and she pressed up against Jane's palm, her nipple hardening. She ran her hands down Jane's neck and fumbled with her shirt buttons.

She kissed each part of Jane's skin as she worked her way down; first the hollow of her collarbone, then between her breasts.

Jane's desire was so intense, it almost hurt.

Kneeling, Amber kissed Jane's belly, pulling her shirt open. Jane pulled it all the way off.

Amber looped her fingers under the waistband of Jane's undies, then pulled them slowly down.

The fire burning through Jane flickered for an instant. Amber was taut, every inch of skin perfect, like she was carved from marble, like a woman in a magazine. *Shit.* Amber had probably been in so many magazines, she had lost count. Jane suddenly felt like a ball of stray hairs and cellulite.

But Amber made a strangled sound in the back of her throat and ran her hands over Jane's naked bum. She pressed her body against Jane's leg and ran her tongue just below her clit.

Heat shot through Jane and blew away any insecurity.

Amber moved her body and mouth against her, groaning again as Jane parted her legs to give better access.

Amber licked slowly but with increasing pressure.

Pleasure radiated through Jane with every movement, but her hands ached with how much she wanted to touch Amber, to give her pleasure as well.

"Let me take you to bed," Jane said, her voice sounding husky and choked to her own ears.

"Please." Amber stood.

Jane reached back and unhooked her own bra.

"Here, let me." Amber removed it and tossed it over the railing. She ran her fingers over Jane's breasts. They were fuller than Amber's, not quite so perfect. Her nipples responded to Amber's touch.

Jane took Amber's hand and led her into the guest bedroom she was using. After switching on a lamp, she turned the covers down and sat on the bed.

Amber stayed standing and moved in between Jane's knees. Amber's skin brushing up her thighs made Jane gasp.

Amber turned and started lowering her undies.

Jane's throat felt thick, but a breathy groan escaped as her eyes roved over Amber's bum.

"Don't touch me yet," said Amber with a smile in her voice.

Jane's hands were on the bed beside her, and they instantly started throbbing with how much she wanted to do the thing she'd just been told not to.

Amber pulled her undies all the way down and kicked them to the side. She started to breathe heavily as she looked over her shoulder at Jane.

Jane balled her hands into fists, gripping the bedsheets as she held herself back.

This made Amber smile.

"You can't touch me. Yet."

Jane's hips bucked against the bed.

Amber ran her fingers over her own collarbone. "OK. I want you to touch me."

Jane moaned and pressed her mouth against the small of Amber's back, her hands caressing her bum then moving around to the front.

Amber gasped as Jane touched her clit. She covered Jane's hand with both of hers and pressed—pressed Jane's fingers hard into herself.

Heat roared between Jane's legs. She pulled Amber onto the bed beside her and straddled her thighs.

Amber responded by spreading her legs wide, spreading Jane's at the same time.

Jane slid a finger inside Amber, groaning at how Amber's back arched.

Amber scrabbled for Jane's torso and pulled her down on top of her, plunging her tongue inelegantly into Jane's mouth. She moved against Jane's hand, pushing her deeper and deeper.

That was it. Jane lost all control. She moaned into Amber's mouth and worked her whole arm rhythmically to give her pleasure.

"Oh God, clit. Clit now," Amber breathed into Jane's ear, clutching the back of her neck.

Jane withdrew and rubbed the wetness over Amber's clit.

Amber gasped. "Oh, yes! Please!" She ran her hand down Jane's belly and touched her with her fingers.

Her hips bucked as she came. She pressed her open mouth to the side of Jane's face and exhaled shakily into her ear. Then she fell back against the pillow, moving the hand that was pressed into Jane's pussy. "Is this OK?" she asked.

Jane nodded, incapable of speech. Amber's movements sent aching heat through her body.

Amber pressed her swollen mouth against Jane's. "I want to taste you."

Jane nodded again and knelt up as Amber scooched out from under her.

Amber ran her hands over Jane's breasts. "Fucking hell, you're perfect. Don't move, stay right there." She moved her head between Jane's knees.

"I'm not kneeling on your hair, am I?" Jane asked.

Her eyes looking up were dark with desire. "You're not, but at this stage I wouldn't even care if you were."

Amber grabbed Jane's bum and lowered her down into her mouth.

Jane threw her head back with a loud moan. She looked down unbelievingly at her own body thrusting and writhing like it had a mind of its own.

Amber's hands squeezed her bum as she licked and sucked.

Jane's orgasm juddered through her like a freight train. She cried out as wave after wave of ecstasy crashed through her.

She collapsed down onto the mattress, limp and heavy and satisfied.

Amber was there in a flash, lying her head nose-to-nose next to Jane's on the pillow.

Jane kissed her lips softly.

Amber scooched in so her body was pressed against Jane's at as many points as possible.

Jane opened her eyes and smiled. A tiny, flickery part deep down in her brain was telling her that this whole thing was impossible. A woman this beautiful and magnetic could not just have had sex with her, touched her, and kissed her with hot desire. At the concert, hundreds of people had been so excited to see Amber and loved her so much that they screamed and jumped around. Nobody felt that way about Jane.

Amber snaked her arm around Jane's rib cage and pulled her even closer, looking into Jane's eyes before kissing the corner of her mouth.

Jane opened her mouth to speak, but no words came out. Every cell in her body glowed with heavy warmth. She had been drawn to Amber, wanted to be as close as possible, and now they were pressed together so tightly that Amber's face in front of hers was almost a blur. And it felt better than even her deepest desires had told her it would.

But the fear still flickered on.

Holding Amber like this felt so *right*.

There was no roadmap for what was going to happen next. She was being told to jump from a plane, unsure that her parachute would work.

Jane took a deep breath, inhaling the scent of Amber, the intermingling of her beauty products' aromas already so familiar.

Jane and her therapist had been working on mindfulness. She closed her eyes and concentrated on the sensation of Amber's smooth skin under her hands. Amber nuzzled her forehead against Jane's cheek.

The flickery voice went away, drowned out by quiet calm and tenderness. She didn't need to decide whether to jump or not. She didn't need to do anything at all.

"Well," whispered Jane. "I certainly got my money's worth for that VIP meet and greet ticket."

She felt Amber smile against her neck.

"You should see what Platinum Class gets you." Amber's voice was muffled by Jane's skin.

Jane smiled too and relaxed into the heavy warmth of afterglow.

"I wanted to kiss you yesterday, downstairs," said Amber, her voice sleepy.

Jane ran her hand down Amber's back and pulled her closer. "I wanted to kiss you too."

"Mmmmmm. That's nice. I wanted you to know I was serious, though—not, you know, playing fast and loose. Coz you're a special lady, Lady Jane." She breathed so deeply, it was almost a snore. "I wanted to take you out. You know, put on the Ritz. All fancy." She patted Jane's cheek.

Jane reached over with the greatest care and switched off the light.

Amber sighed like a comfortable puppy as Jane wrapped her up in her arms again. "Can I tell you a secret?" she whispered.

"Yes," Jane whispered back. Every part of her body was warm, snuggly, and contented.

"The book—about taking surveys, and research and...equilibrium? It's bad." She creased her forehead and closed her eyes even tighter. "Very, very boring. And complicated! You know what? I never even wanted it one bit. I was using the dumb book as an excuse to be alone with you." Amber's breath feathered across Jane's cheek as she giggled.

It tickled in the best way.

Amber grew still and heavy as she fell asleep.

Jane brushed her forehead with a kiss and lay for a while, smiling.

CHAPTER 13

Amber woke up to noise and frantic movement. She reached sideways. The bed was empty. *Strange.* Someone was meant to be there.

Jane!

Loud repetitive chiming assaulted her ears, and too-bright sunshine made her squint.

"Shit. Shit!" a voice said. *Jane's voice.*

Amber's eyes adjusted, and Jane's outline came into focus, sitting naked on the edge of the bed, holding her phone, which was ringing loudly.

Amber sprang to Jane's side. "What's going on?"

Jane shook the phone in her face. "It's Sara. She made me get WhatsApp, and now she's calling me on it." She had to almost shout over the noise.

"Decline the call if you don't want to talk to her."

"I'm trying! Is it swipe or—shit!!"

The ringing stopped. Amber saw a split second of someone's face filling the screen before Jane flung her phone across the room. It landed face down on the carpet.

Amber snorted with laughter.

Jane pressed her fingers to her lips, eyes darting wildly.

Amber clapped both hands over her mouth, trying to stop her chuckles escaping.

"Hello, Jane? Hello?" Sara's voice from the phone could barely be heard from where it had landed.

Jane padded towards it, like it was a bomb or poisonous snake. She knelt down next to it.

Great bum. Amber got comfy on the bed, stretching out and propping herself up by the elbow so she could look at Jane. Geez, she really had a nice arse. Strong and generous. Amber had admired it a number of times over the past few days—in jeans, or slacks—but the unencumbered view was even better.

"H-hello. Sara? Can you hear me?"

"Yah. Kind of. But I can't see you. Are you inside a cupboard?"

"No, um, I bought the wrong phone case. From Koreatown, you know? And it's covering up my camera. And microphone too, I guess."

"Huh?" Even though Amber could barely hear Sara, she could tell she was unconvinced.

Amber snorted again.

Jane shot her a look over her shoulder.

Amber raised her eyebrows and shook her head. *If you want me to stop laughing, stop being hilarious.*

"Are you with someone?" Sara asked.

"No! No-one at all. I have a podcast on. ABC Radio National, covering question time in the Senate."

"The Senate's sitting on New Year's Day?"

"Well, no. It's an old episode. One of my favourites."

"Oh, right. Well, I just called to wish you a happy new year."

"Thank you, sweetie. Let me fix my phone, and I'll call you back in a little bit, OK?"

"OK, talk then."

Jane waited a few seconds after silence fell. Amber could see her rib cage moving as she breathed hard.

Finally, she turned the phone over with a quick movement and only picked it up once she was certain the call had disconnected.

Amber watched Jane walk back towards her. She felt a dull throb of arousal. Jane's breasts swung slightly as she walked, again generous and full. The memory of last night flooded back into her brain, turning her on even more.

Jane didn't get back under the covers. She sat down hunched over instead.

Amber clutched the pillowcase. An anxious flutter started up in her chest.

A daydream played through her mind, of her and Jane in bathrobes, tousled and mussed hair just like now, sipping coffee, laughing and talking loudly to Sara through a device propped up on the kitchen counter.

The image vanished as Amber watched Jane now, controlling her breathing, like she was trying to recover from a trauma.

The stark opposite of the little Hallmark movie snippet in her mind.

The difference was jarring. *OK, so I'm not a psycho.* She knew the ease and familiarity of her daydream wouldn't come about immediately. She didn't spend one amazing night with someone and want to be in total domestic bliss with them the very next day.

But did Jane have to seem quite so devastated at a family member nearly springing her in bed with Amber? Like it was a shameful crime?

"What's up?" Amber said. She wanted Jane to look at her.

Jane's face was pale as she turned. "Oh, sorry." She took a breath and shook her shoulders. "I got discombobulated with the phone ringing so loud. I get frustrated when technology doesn't work for me. It makes me feel old." She pressed her lips into a small smile.

"Really?" She knew her voice was as cold as steel.

Jane's smile vanished.

Tone it down, Hatfield. Nobody likes a morning-after psycho in their bedroom.

Jane put her phone on the bedside table. She sat on the bed and looked Amber full in the face. "To tell you the truth, I struggle when I feel I'm not in control of situations. Like everything is a house of cards that's going to topple if even one thing doesn't go absolutely to plan. You might have met people like that before, but my autism can make me even more rigid than usual.

"It's not that I don't want Sara to know that we've been, well, spending time together, but I would want to tell her in my own way and in my own time. I'm sorry I wasn't honest with you a moment ago. I don't usually lie."

Amber took Jane's hand. "It's me who should apologise. I've got my own stuff. Um..."

Should she tell her? Jane's total honesty felt like swimming in cool water on a hot, sticky day. Pure relief. Could she do the same?

Amber swallowed. "I act badly when I feel rejected. I, uh, I don't have any contact with my mum anymore. I grew up completely intertwined with her; she was a single mum, you know—and a bit of a stage mum, in hindsight. When I was doing well, booking gigs, getting agency meetings, making money, she was great to be around. We had fun. But when things didn't go right—when I did something 'wrong'—she would withhold. Withhold everything: affection, attention...love. She wouldn't even look at me. She'd go away, and I wouldn't know where she was or when she was coming back.

"But that's not your fault. I've worked for a long time on not being defensive or snippy when I perceive rejection. And not making it my life's purpose to avoid rejection."

She passed her hand over her eyes. "Phew! Sorry! It's a lot, I know." She was exposed and had an urge to hide—to paper over her discomfort and Jane's. To make it all right.

Jane squeezed her hand. "Thanks for explaining. Thank you." Her eyes glowed with a steady warmth.

Amber nodded, her throat tight. To be seen and accepted by this person, a relative stranger, felt huge. *Not a stranger.* Although she had only known Jane a few days, something inside her recognised that this was much more than a passing fling.

Jane smiled. "My niece nearly started her year out by seeing my knockers. Near miss for her."

Amber chuckled and ran her hand down Jane's cheek, resting it on her collarbone. "Glad it's not a near miss for me. My resolution was to see as many knockers as possible. Oh crap, I've got make-up all over your pillowcases." She propped herself up to assess the damage.

Jane snuggled in under the covers and put her arms around Amber, pulling her down next to her. "Don't worry about it. Knowing my sister, this is some hi-tech organic bamboo something-or-other bed linen. Probably self-cleaning. Plus, you know how the old oft-quoted phrase goes?"

"Which one's that?"

"Worth it!"

Amber laughed.

Jane had hit her punchline way too hard. Definitely had not pulled it off. But it was downright adorable. She kissed her, slipping in some cheeky tongue.

Jane returned the kiss, running her hand down and boldly grabbing Amber's bum.

Amber giggled. "Watch you getting fresh, Professor."

"Not a professor yet. Just a doctor." She hadn't taken her hand away from the butt cheek.

Amber sighed. What was it about Jane that made her feel she could stay cuddled up under these covers with her forever? She was all lit up from the inside. But Jane's pale misery only moments before played in the back of her mind.

She cleared her throat. *Whatever!* A great first official date, fantastic sex, and morning cuddles—it didn't mean she needed Jane to vow that they would grow old together. *Keep it light. Keep it fun.* If she had her heart broken (and it wouldn't be the first time), it wouldn't kill her. "How long are you in town again?"

"I fly out on the third. The day after tomorrow."

Can't you stay longer? It was too soon. It was unhinged to have feelings this big so quickly.

"Do you reckon you could make some time for me?" she said instead.

"I reckon I could squeeze you in," Jane said, holding her close and wrapping her strong legs around her tightly.

Amber grinned, delight bubbling up inside her. Jane, who was laced up so tight, taking every aspect of her life seriously, was *funny.* And generous and passionate. She was like a wonderful secret only Amber knew about.

She relaxed into Jane's body. She must have felt this comfortable with people before, but she couldn't remember when.

The day after tomorrow. She sighed. *I might be in a spot of trouble here.* But life was for the living, not running and hiding from theoretical future heartbreaks. She wiggled her hips to place herself more firmly between Jane's legs.

"Careful, you're going to get me going again," whispered Jane.

"Duh. That's the whole point."

CHAPTER 14

Jane spent most of New Year's Day in bed. She made Amber an omelette for lunch, and Amber made pasta with random fridge vegetables for dinner. At one stage, Jane scrounged around in her sister's en suite for heavy duty make-up remover for Amber, to prevent someone named Fabia being concerned about Amber's pores, apparently.

In the evening, they sat rugged up with a blanket on their knees, Selena on Amber's lap and glasses of wine in hand in the garden, before heading back up to Jane's bed in the guest room.

The next morning, she woke up to a pinging notification on her phone. There was a groan next to her, and she squinted her eyes open against the late-morning sunlight, wondering who was there in her groggy half-dream state.

A mess of long hair.

Jane closed her eyes again and smiled. *Amber.*

Her phone pinged again, even though she had all the pings turned off for her apps. She reached for the phone in slow motion, so as not to wake Amber.

Maybe it was Sara again, checking up on her via some new wacky app that Jane didn't even know the name of. She had a twinge of unease, remembering the flurry of embarrassment the morning before brought on by Sara's New Year's call.

In the moment, she had almost been paralysed by panic. Not being able to work the app properly had thrown her, made her feel not in control of the situation. But it was more than that. The possibility of Sara knowing about Amber had panicked her. Sara would be carried away with ecstatic excitement and probably start shopping online for a pearly white bridal tuxedo for Jane's nuptials. Then, when this fling was over and Amber's friendly text messages from the other side of the world finally dried up, Sara would look at her sadly, and Barbara and Bill would look at her sadly, and her mum and dad would look at her sadly, and they would all think how magical it would have been if Jane had managed to make it work. This time.

Jane unlocked her phone to see the stacked collection of notifications from the airline. Check-in was open via the app. Twenty-four hours until departure. Time to upgrade now for Economy Plus.

She slumped back down and lay staring at the ceiling. *Twenty-four hours.* All dreams had to be woken up from. Even ultrarealistic ones that made the dreamer feel deep things they didn't think they were capable of anymore.

Amber sighed in her sleep, crinkled her nose, and snorted gently as if she were a quieter and much cuter version of the Peppa Pig character Sara had loved so much as a toddler.

Jane wanted to smile and frown at the same time. An ache started behind her eyes. In twenty-four hours, was she never going to see this face again? What was the alternative—would Amber declare that she wanted Jane to be her girlfriend after less than a week? When their first actual date had been, what, two days ago? Maybe Jane could give up her career and do Mr Hairdo's job. Cash in hand, of course, because she didn't have a green card.

Amber opened her eyes, squinted, and blinked. She smiled as they focused finally on Jane's face. "Good morning."

Jane's ache got worse. "Hi."

The smile was replaced with a forehead crease. "What's wrong?"

"Nothing. Nothing's wrong." She held up her phone. "Online check-in's open. For my flight. I was worried the notifications would disturb you."

"Oh." Amber ran her fingertips over Jane's cheek, pausing at the outer corner of her eye and mouth, just where she was holding all her tension from the happy/sad battle going on inside her. "Hey, now, no need to worry."

Jane exhaled in a puff. She felt a little better.

"Look, we've got the whole day together. Let's put a glass dome over it."

"Heh?"

Amber's laugh tinkled. "I hope you're better at interrogating theories and ideas with articulate questions at your fancy university." She sat up and mimed pulling a giant hat the size of two woks down over the top of them. "The dome protects us from the past, the future, other people—we don't have to worry about any of that. We just exist together, here and now. It's radical mindfulness."

Jane imagined the dome, with one shining day inside it, cut off from the swirling chaos outside. It was a calm image. "I like the dome. Can I be honest, though?"

A shadow of the eyebrow crease returned. "Of course you can."

"I'm really just lying here staring at your knockers. Is making out allowed in the dome?"

She grinned. "It most certainly is."

Jane pulled Amber down on top of her and kissed her. She cupped one of the knockers and the nipple hardened against her palm.

Amber squealed. "OK, OK, OK. I have to wee so bad!" She jumped up, wheeled around and pointed a finger at Jane. "Don't you dare go anywhere. I will be right back."

Jane raised her palms in surrender. "I won't move a muscle. You're the boss."

"Ooooh, I like that. One sec." She bounded into the en suite bathroom. "What do you want to do for dome day?" she shouted through the closed door.

Jane put her hands behind her head on the pillow and stretched. "I had a list going of some things I wanted to do this week. There was one thing in particular that a colleague on the architecture faculty recommended, if you wouldn't mind?"

The door opened. "I'm down for anything or any place, as long as you're there too," said Amber.

Jane reached for her hand as she neared the bed and pulled her back down into the sheets. "You're sweet. Now, it would be rude of me to do anything else before I've paid my proper respects to these knockers."

"It's a true miracle," said Amber as she closed the car door. "On-street parking downtown in the middle of the day."

"I guess the second day of the year is the time to come."

Amber looked around at the almost-deserted street. "Will it even be open?"

"Yes, it's open. Americans don't believe in paid time off for workers. Not like back home."

Amber nodded. "All right, where now?"

They set off down the footpath. Amber took hold of Jane's arm and leant into her. The brown office buildings on either side of the street created a chilly wind tunnel. A cardboard party hat with *Happy New Year!* written on it blew past them. It was so quiet, they could hear it bop along the concrete as it cartwheeled away.

The buildings gave way to a square of brownish grass and tall, spindly palm trees. They crossed the square along a broad pathway towards their destination.

Above a set of grand arches, *Los Angeles City Hall* was written in brass letters, just below a line of flags jutting out from the building's face. Above the arches, a grand building rose thirty-two stories high.

Amber squeezed Jane's arm then ran ahead of her up the wide stone steps. "This is so cool! I feel like so many movie scenes were shot here. I can picture it."

"I'm sure they were. My friend Philomena says the building is a wonderful example of Art Deco design. They wanted a grand structure that was ancient Rome for the modern empire."

Amber looked up. "They did a good job. When was it built?"

"The late 1920s. There was a lot of prosperity and optimism in the US at the time. Idealism, even. Society had made it through World War I. They didn't know the Great Depression was right around the corner."

Amber came back down the steps and took Jane's hand. "You can see it, can't you. The hope."

They stood side-by-side for a moment until the wind gusted and they both climbed the stairs again at a run.

Through the arches and inside a high-ceilinged lobby, a young man behind a wooden desk put down his phone as their footsteps echoed through the big space.

"Hello," said Jane. "We'd like to look around, if that's OK?"

"Yes! Thank goodness. Wonderful. I thought you might have been here to get married, and that's a lot more paperwork."

Amber snickered. "Have you brought me here under false pretences, Jane?"

Anxiety crackled in Jane's head before she remembered the dome. *No past, no future.* She grinned. "Would it be so bad if I had? We've got nothing else to do today."

"True, true." She furrowed her brow and put a finger to her chin. "Look, Teddy will kill me if I get married without letting him sell the story to *New Idea* magazine, but maybe"—she squinted at the receptionist's name tag—"Deacon here could take some photos on my phone?"

Deacon's mouth dropped open.

Jane looked sideways at Amber, and they both cracked up giggling. "Sorry, Deacon. Just the self-guided tour after all, please."

Deacon cleared his throat. "Sign here, and here," he said, then handed them each a thin piece of paper not much bigger than a credit card. "These are your passes. You need to keep them with you while you're in the building. And hand them back to me on your way out. And here's an information booklet."

"Thank you, Deacon," they said in unison before leaving the lobby and entering a slightly smaller room with a double staircase leading grandly upwards.

"He didn't sound so thrilled about having to interact with us again on our way out," said Amber, the laughter still in her voice.

"I agree. He looked at us like we were pair of aunts whose jokes weren't funny."

"Not to mention borderline offensive!"

Jane took Amber's hand as they mounted the staircase. She referred to the booklet. "There's a wooden lift that was installed in 1928, but it's no longer in use."

"Ahh, yeah. I don't have a phobia, but I wouldn't ride a 100-year-old lift even if your book said it was fine."

"Fair. OK, if we take the stairs to the sixth floor, there's a lift we can use there to get us to the observation deck at the top."

"And when was that lift put in?"

"1997."

"Oof. No worries. I'm sure I've ridden in older without knowing it. Fly me to the moon, Captain!"

They meandered their way up, peeking into rooms on every floor. They didn't see another person as they wandered about. Through a long window, they looked into a lovely old meeting room, wood panelled, with high-backed leather office chairs around a large oval table.

Amber tried the handle, and the door opened without a sound. "It feels like we shouldn't be allowed in all these oldy-timey rooms. They feel opulent," Amber whispered as she entered, Jane close behind her. Amber sat down at the head of the table. She put on an old Hollywood reporter's voice. "Now, just you see here, Mr Roosevelt, you're talking screwy. Just screwy, I tell ya!"

Jane sat down as well. "You see here, doll face! You won't razzle-dazzle the Charleston on this caboose, you hear?"

Amber snorted. "This leather feels like butter," she said, returning to her normal voice. She ran her hands along both armrests. Her eyes met Jane's, and she stood up. "Did you feel it?" She sat in Jane's lap, as side-on at the buttery armrests would allow.

Jane tensed, but then mentally pulled the dome down more firmly over the whole of downtown LA. She gave the leather chair back above her shoulder a cursory graze with her knuckle. "Eh, upholstery's not really my thing. *This,* however..." she said running her hands from Amber's knees up to the small of her back, under her jacket but over her jumper and a couple of other layers, "is the cat's pyjamas."

Amber cupped Jane's face and kissed her, slowly and with purpose.

Jane pulled her body closer by her hips, and deepened the kiss. Every cell in Jane's body felt good, like she was swirling around in pure pleasure. Amber's body under her hands was perfect, like touching her was what Jane was born to do. Her hand pressed against Amber's inner thigh, and Amber's hips pressed into Jane's lap with a new urgency.

They broke the kiss at the same time.

Amber gave a sheepish smile. "Deacon's probably watching on the security cameras. We had better stop before I start begging you to lay me out right on this historical table."

Jane nodded. "Yes. He might not recover from seeing his old aunts doing that."

"Hah! Yes, think of the therapy bills." She intertwined her fingers with Jane's and grasped her hand. "Let's look at this hopeful building some more."

"Excellent idea." She cleared her throat, then leaned in close. "Then what say I lay you out back at home, doll face?"

"Hot diggity dog!"

They didn't see another living soul on any of the other floors, in the 1997 lift, or out on the observation deck. It was like Amber had manifested the glass dome into physical existence, and it was sitting on top of the old skyscraper.

Amber leaned against the railing, the wind whipping her hair. The sun was out, and the city was sprawled below them, with white, beige, and grey downtown buildings scattered around in a palm tree-lined grid. She gasped and pointed, "Look, the Hollywood sign. How cool!"

Jane wrapped her in her arms from behind and pressed her cheek to hers. "There it is."

Amber ran her hand up and rested it against the hairline at the back of Jane's neck.

Sadness tugged at Jane, but she concentrated on the rise and fall of Amber's chest as she breathed. In and out. Did she imagine it, or could she feel the flutter of Amber's pulse against her own neck?

Everyone—Sara, Barbara, even architecture-obsessed Philomena—assumed Jane would be spending today alone. The second day of the new year. She had thought so too. Her week alone in the wintry city played on a reel in her head. She would have come here by herself and got the booklet from Deacon, and one set of footsteps would have echoed through the grand cavernous spaces of the municipal building.

The loneliness and greyness of that "sliding doors" week seemed to seep out into her entire life. Each day she went to work, chatted with colleagues, avoided Lauren, and spent her allocated hours teaching the students. She enjoyed elements of it, of course. Spontaneous debates that caught like wildfire in her tutorials, and those moments of alchemy when a young person changed her own long-held perspective on something—those filled her cup and told her she was in the right profession.

This week, her emotions had swelled like a full-volume symphony. Joy, desire, attraction, pleasure—they had filled her body right up. She was in technicolour.

She held onto Amber a little tighter. It wasn't this wonderful, funny, giving woman's fault that Jane wasn't fulfilled in her life and would be lonely without her.

The greatest gift Jane could give her was a goodbye with no obligations.

Amber was sweet all the way through. If she knew how much of a difference she had made to Jane, and how cold and empty her normal life now seemed in comparison, she might try to fix it. She might promise something that was impossible to give—a life together. The symphony playing all the time. But it was a fantasy.

Things didn't end up that way for people like Jane.

"I can feel you thinking," said Amber. She pressed her lips to Jane's cheek. "Too much thinking isn't allowed in the dome."

"Sorry. You're right. No thinking, only looking."

"And hugging. That's allowed."

Jane wished on the LA Freeway, Union Station, and Disney Music Hall that she could freeze time. Eventually Amber's teeth started chattering, and they headed back to the lift.

CHAPTER 15

LAX airport loomed into Jane's view, rising out of the desert-brown landscape, huge and ugly.

They had decided the parameters. Amber would drive Jane to the airport. She would drop her at the departures areas. She wouldn't park. She wouldn't come in.

It had been a feat to convince Sara that she couldn't drop her off. "The traffic will be terrible for you on the way back," she had said. Sara had argued harder, forcing Jane to say she wanted a chance to improve her Lyft passenger rating, because she had spilt tea in another Lyft and she was worried about getting tanked. Plus, Sara and Barbara and Bill had just gotten back from the airport not long before. Sara had pouted but finally conceded.

Jane had left Amber's house in the early chill hours of the morning, welcomed her family home, told them complete and utter lies about the last six days, and then taken a Lyft all the way back to Amber's house. Now Amber was in the driver's seat of her tiny purple electric car.

She put her hand on Amber's thigh.

Amber patted the hand, then gripped the steering wheel again. The traffic *was* terrible (making one of Jane's lies to Sara true).

Jane yawned. She hadn't slept much the night before. She had lain awake for what felt like hours, listening to Amber's slow breathing and thinking about how she was more beautiful, more magical, than even her most adoring fans could have imagined.

Jane looked over at her and smiled, then whipped her head back around as the pressure of tears built up behind her eyes.

They had each other's contact details, sure. One might send the other a cute text, or a meme that referenced a shared joke, but Jane didn't expect promises of anything more.

She didn't want Amber to be weighed down.

"You'll text me as soon as you land?" Amber asked.

"Yes." There should have been a term of endearment added to her response. She heard the absence of it. What would she call Amber, if they were a couple. Babe? Honey? She bit her lip. *Dangerous thoughts.*

The air traffic control tower appeared on the left, and cold dread spread through Jane. Was this all wrong?

Stay strong. Amber was an empath. If Jane asked her for some kind of commitment, there was a chance Amber would give it. Even "look me up when you're in town next" was problematic. Amber might mean it in the moment, yes, but that wouldn't make it the right decision. Would Jane expect her to stop looking for her real Mrs Right in the meantime? Logic had to win out here.

Eight days ago, I didn't know she existed, now I'm having trouble imagining not being with her.

Impulsive, emotion-driven decisions were what got people into trouble. She had seen it time and time again.

Amber pulled into the drop-and-go zone, three lanes deep with cars stopped at zany angles. She wove her little car deftly in and out to pull up in a coveted space next to the curb.

Duelling car horns blared a discordant and deafening soundtrack. Signs with big, red letters bombarded Jane with instructions: *Drivers must stay with the car. No Parking. No idling. Two-minute maximum. Fines and penalties apply.*

Jane didn't want to move. She didn't want to put her hand on the car door handle because it meant that she was leaving Amber behind. She would probably never see her again.

She heard Amber's car door and lifted her head. Amber went around and grabbed Jane's luggage from the boot.

Jane hurried around to help her.

"I got this, Jane. I'm stronger than I look." She took the little carry-on, then the big suitcase over to the curb with surprising ease.

Jane shook her head. "You think I would have learned by now not to underestimate you."

They stood facing each other.

A quick goodbye. That's what Jane had stipulated she wanted when they'd discussed this the night before. Their fling should be a happy memory, not something to sadly regret.

Jane pulled Amber to her, hugging her close.

Amber wrapped her arms around Jane's middle, pressing her lips to her neck.

Amber looked up at her, her bottom lip starting to wobble.

"Oh no! Don't be unhappy!" Jane said.

Amber took a step back. "Just listen. I'm not going to get this out if I don't go fast. Look, you've made it very clear that you want this to be the end of us. Yeah, amicable, sure. No hard feelings. An affair to remember. All that." She reached out and took Jane's hand. She gestured with her other hand to encompass the aggressive cars, shouting people, and the giant automatic doors waiting to close behind Jane in a few moments. "But this, all this, sucks. There's no way to avoid it sucking."

"Ma'am! Excuse me ma'am. No idling, please. You gotta move this vehicle along," an airport cop said, standing unnecessarily close to them.

Amber turned a 7000-watt smile on him. "Of course! I'll be out of here in just a jiffy, sir. Thank you so much."

He rocked back on his heels a little and tipped his hat. "No problems at all ma'am. You have yourself a great day." He moved on to shout at a family with four small children trying to get half a dozen suitcases out of a minivan.

"Where was I?" Amber asked.

"This sucks."

"Oh yeah. And maybe you're right. What if we try to keep this going and it's hard and awkward and we fizzle out and the time difference is confusing? That would be bad, but..." She held Jane's face in both her hands. "I think it's worth not cutting this off. You don't want to make any promises, sure, I can go along with that. But what if I come and see you? In a few months? I really don't want this to be the end for us."

Jane reeled, her brain spinning. Her instincts told her to stick to the plan, to be stoic, to accept that she couldn't have what she wanted.

A shining tear spilled and ran down Amber's cheek.

Jane's convictions crumbled down like a wrecking ball had gone through them. She looked into Amber's eyes. "Yes, of course. Come and visit me. I would love that."

More tears cascaded. "Oh, shit yeah! Good result," she said and pressed her mouth to Jane's.

Jane held her close and returned the kiss. *I'm an idiot who doesn't know anything.* Her chest burst with tenderness, and she wrapped Amber up even more tightly. *I convinced myself to walk away from this, from her.* Jane swore to herself that she would do better. Sure, there was no clear line of logic through to a satisfactory conclusion. Maybe a satisfactory conclusion was impossible, no matter how well she planned. But feelings meant something. She glowed with warmth and joy, and if that wasn't the point of living, then what was?

Amber gave the airport cop who had finally gotten stern enough to force her to let Jane go a little wave as she launched her car back into the madness of LAX traffic. Happiness zinged around in her belly. She had made a big swing and avoided the goodbye that would have crushed her.

She tapped her car screen a few times and, after a few rings, Teddy's voice came through the speakers.

"Amber, hey! How did you go at the airport?"

"Teddy, you have to get me to Australia. For as long as possible."

He gasped. "But, you know what that means."

"I know."

"You said you would never! You said it was the last resort of the damned. One step below career purgatory."

"I know what I said."

"Amber, are you sure?"

"I'm sure. Make the call." She gripped the wheel tighter. "Make me a celebrity judge on an Australian television singing contest."

"Consider it done." He hung up.

Brown and grey airport surroundings were morphing into brown and grey industrial buildings punctuated with colourful billboards promoting new seasons of trashy reality TV.

"I'm going away for a while," she whispered to the city. "I hope it's worth it."

CHAPTER 16

Three months later

Sara plopped down into a beat-up office chair and turned two full spins. "Yeah, wow, it's really, um, great," she said.

Jane grinned. She had been looking forward to showing Sara her office while her niece was in Brisbane for a short visit. College spring break coincided with a business trip to Brisbane for Barbara, and Sara was only too happy to take advantage of a small percentage of her mum's many frequent flyer miles.

The last time Sara had visited her at the uni, Jane had a been sharing a desk in the faculty staff room with a semiretired tutor named Mervyn, who often forgot which days he was meant to be working. She had spent a lot of time marking papers in the library.

"You don't think it needs any, you know, personal touches, though? There's nothing that embodies your essence in here."

"There's books," said Jane. "And bound copies of all the research papers and journal articles I've authored."

"Mmmm," said Sara, performing another twirl. She put her index finger to her chin. "Maybe a poster? Of something you really like? Um." She scrunched up her face. "The Collections and Research Centre at the Queensland Museum! I'm not sure they sell posters of it, but if you took a photo, I could get one made."

"Hmmmm," said Jane. She wasn't following what her niece was saying as closely as usual. Something else was on her mind. She huffed out a shallow breath.

"What's up? Are you OK?" asked Sara.

Jane's throat felt tight. She had been looking forward to this, had been talking to Amber for the last few days about doing it. But now that it came down to it, it was like her mouth wouldn't do her bidding. She had never liked letting cats out of bags, even when they were friendly cats that everyone enjoyed seeing. Even those were notoriously difficult to get back *in* the bag if there were unforeseen consequences.

In the time that had gone by since Jane had left LA, she and Amber had been in touch almost every day. When she got home from work, Jane would call Amber and they would talk. Not always about big things, just what was going on, people they'd seen, funny questions Jane's students had asked her.

If their LA fling had been an impossible accident that Jane could explain away, this new remote relationship was much more deliberate.

It was real, and Jane wanted to make it feel more real.

She cleared her throat. "Sara, I want to talk to you about something."

"Ooooooo. Something good, I hope?"

"Yes, um, you remember when we went to the VIP meet and greet?"

"With Amber Hatfield, Jane. Don't tell me you've forgotten her name again."

Jane's mouth twitched. *OK, maybe this is a little bit fun.* "No, no I haven't. Well, as we were leaving the venue, her assistant gave me Amber's phone number."

Sara's jaw dropped. She covered her mouth in both her hands. "I *knew* it. I knew it! You were in there, charming as hell, making her laugh. She picked up what you were putting down! What happened? Tell me, tell me, tell me!" She bounced up from the chair and grabbed Jane's forearms, putting her wide-eyed face very close.

Jane shook her head in amazement. "You're so quick to believe something was going to happen. I'm still not sure I believe it."

"*A-doi.* You're a total catch. What don't I believe? What happened?"

Jane cocked her head to the side. "Hmmmm, let me see if I can recall." *Yes, all right. This is a lot fun.*

Sara squeezed tighter.

"Ouch! All right! I texted her, and she asked if we could meet for coffee, and I said yes."

Sara started jumping up and down on the spot, letting out a little "eep!" every time she landed.

"Then we had another date after that and spent quite a bit of time together while I was house-sitting."

"Oh. My. God!" She was getting out of breath from the jumping.

"What's the hot news?" said a voice with an English accent.

Sara stopped bouncing and swung around. "Oh, it's you," she said.

"Hello, Lauren," said Jane.

Lauren blinked at Sara as she entered the small room. "Hello, pet. It's good to see you again."

"Hi."

The oxygen was sucked out of the room. Jane could almost hear the *whoomph!*

Lauren surveyed her a moment longer as if expecting her to say something more. Her shoulder-length, perfectly straight hair barely undulated as she turned from Sara to Jane, then back again. "So, what's got you both giddy with excitement? You know I hate to be left out."

Jane swallowed. Of course it was Lauren ruining this moment. It seemed so natural.

Near the end of their relationship, Lauren's sole purpose had been to make Jane feel bad. It wasn't until Lauren had finally pulled the pin that Jane had even realised it. It made her stomach twist to think how long she had let it go on.

She shook her shoulders. Today was a great day. And Lauren didn't have the same effect on her as before, especially since LA. She still had to see her most days at work, but their run-ins didn't affect her like they used to.

In fact, Jane had said hi to Lauren in the hall the day before and had walked another few metres before realising that it didn't have any emotional effect on her. She had been thinking about a story Amber had told her about a fan who had screen-printed all her album covers onto a cushion and sent it to her. Amber had asked if Sara maybe wanted it.

"We were just..." Jane said. She didn't like telling lies, and even more, she hated that Lauren was forcing her into telling a lie. *Why don't you mind your own beeswax?* Come to think of it, Lauren had been initiating conversations with Jane more and more the last couple of weeks. Her approaches started off friendly enough, but there was always a sting in the tail.

"Jane has taken up pickleball," said Sara in a rush.

Lauren's eyes narrowed. She looked from Sara to Jane. "Really?"

Jane thought this "news" wouldn't have warranted the excitement from Sara that Lauren had walked in on.

Sara must have realised the same thing, because she continued, "Yes! Yep. And I'm stoked for her, because she's playing in the, um, amateur Pan-Pacific, uh, over-35s Tournament of Champions." She smiled weakly at Jane.

Jane clenched her jaw. She appreciated Sara's effort to help her out, but this was going to be a big, ongoing lie to maintain. Especially if Lauren told other university staff. Jane foresaw a tragic amateur-pickleball-career-ending injury in her near future. Maybe an ankle? But she would have to remember to limp. Neck? The chemist did sell braces...

Lauren clasped her hands together in front of her. "Wow, that's wonderful, Jane. A tad surprising, though."

Sara rolled her eyes at Jane behind Lauren's back.

Jane scratched her nose to hide a grin.

She wasn't going to bite.

The silence lengthened.

Jane really didn't want to know Lauren's opinion on her new, fake all-consuming hobby, but she also wanted this conversation to be over. "Why surprising?"

Sara gave her a mock scowl for giving in so quickly.

Lauren took a deep breath. "Well, if you think about it, the selection panel for the associate professor position is looking for someone with real commitment to the university and the students. A new hobby—one that you've gotten so good at that you're playing a big tournament—well, let's just say I'm surprised that it's a choice you're making right now."

Jane's face went hot. Her mind spun with the image of Lauren whispering in the staff room about how Jane wasn't serious about the job. It wouldn't be the first time Lauren had tried to undermine her. The frustrating thing was how readily her colleagues were willing to believe the worst about her. The university was full of people with imposter syndrome looking for any chance to boost themselves up by pulling other people down.

She opened her mouth to speak, but Lauren wasn't done.

"I know how badly you want this promotion. You always dedicated everything to this job." She tucked her hair behind one ear and glanced up and out of the window before continuing in a small voice. "Everything, at the expense of other things. Important things."

Jane's arms fell to her sides. *This again.* The same old story. That Jane had become distant and mean, a stranger in her own house. That she had driven Lauren away, ignored her, until Lauren had no choice but to end it and escape with the little dignity she had left.

She had peddled this story to Jane's colleagues and friends and had even phoned Jane's parents on more than one occasion, on the pretence of being concerned about Jane's mental state, but actually to tell them a string of stories about her neglectful treatment of Lauren.

When really it was Lauren who had changed without warning—started picking arguments and finding fault with Jane wherever she could. Lauren had eventually broken up with her, with no explanation that made any sense. She had spent months in counselling trying to piece it all together.

Sara's opinion was that Lauren had gotten bored and wanted some drama in her life. Jane hadn't believed it at first. It was too painful to think the woman she had been with for nearly fifteen years, made a home with, loved, could be capable of that. But as the months went by, Jane was starting to think she couldn't rule the theory out completely.

"Thanks for stopping by," said Sara. Her voice was cold.

Lauren blinked at her.

Sara lifted her hand and gave a slow wave.

Lauren threw a look over her shoulder at Jane, as if asking her to step in.

Jane stood stony.

"It was lovely to see you Sara," said Lauren, moving towards the door.

"Enjoy the rest of your day," replied Sara, again with so little warmth, she sounded like dodgy AI.

Jane and Sara stood with their heads inclined to the door for a few moments, making sure her footsteps had fully receded.

"Deadset mole," said Sara finally. "Her only qualification for being an English lecturer is that she's English. And I reckon she's been bunging on that fake posh accent this whole time."

Jane scoffed and shook her head, giving Sara's arm a squeeze. Her family, especially her sister and niece, had gotten her through. Lauren had gaslit her so badly that she had started to believe her own actions had ruined her relationship. A bit of Sara perspective always put Jane right, though.

"Now, where were we? Oh, right. What the actual fuck? You had a Hollywood affair with Amber Freakin' Hatfield! OMG! Have you seen her since?"

Jane shook her head.

"When are you seeing her again?"

She grinned at how much Sara was going to hit the roof. For weeks, wave after wave of excitement had been crashing inside her at the thought of seeing Amber again, and now it could actually have an outlet. "Soon, actually. Next Tuesday. I'm accompanying her to the APRA Music Awards in Sydney."

Sara's face formed a frozen soundless scream. She clasped her head.

"Now, don't get carried away. Lauren was right, only to a certain extent, of course. I don't want this to be a big distraction as I'm going for this associate professor vacancy. It's all I've ever wanted."

Sara bit down on her bottom lip and screwed up her face.

Jane chuckled. "It's OK, you can say it."

She exhaled loudly as if she'd been forced to hold her breath. "I know you want to be a professor here really bad. You love this place, I get it." She glanced around at the scruffy nineties office furniture as if she didn't, in fact, get it. "But it seems crazy to only have eyes for this job you *want* when you've *got* Amber Freakin' Hatfield."

Jane's insides prickled. She had thrown herself so entirely into this race for the promotion, it had kept her afloat when every other aspect of her life was on fire. Now flames seemed to ebb around the vision she had held so close to her heart: an associate professorship at the state's top university, her parents proud of her, a winner rising triumphant from the wreckage of her failed relationship.

She nodded slowly. It was worth holding onto, this career dream. Amber lit her up from the inside, but she was still an unknown at the end of the day. When she was on the other side of the world, it was at times easier to believe Jane was still a whim for her, a mad fancy she would get over all of a sudden.

If Jane worked hard enough, she would get this job. It was a process, there were rules. Emotions wouldn't take it away from her. She would win it fair and square.

Sara strode over and took her by the shoulders. "You do got her, don't you Aunt Jane? Tell me you got her?"

Jane laughed and stepped sideways. "Don't shake me in my workplace! I'll call campus security. Look, I don't know anything about if I've 'got' Amber or not. It's all very new. And long-distance relationships are hard. I like her, though." Her face went hot.

Like her. Like? Jane didn't enjoy it when words were inadequate to describe facts or situations. These last few months since she'd gotten back from LA, she'd carried Amber in her back pocket like a good-luck charm. Or a container of sunshine. She could reach in and access glowing happiness whenever she wanted. But Amber was so far away. Sometimes she had flashes of panic that her feelings existed in a vacuum and were completely one-sided.

"Eeeeee! I could die. This is absolutely the best thing that has ever happened in the history of the universe."

"Careful. I'll be in big trouble with your parents if you die on my watch. Shall we go and have some lunch?"

"Yes, I'm starved. I can't get over all of this. It's surreal. What are you going to wear on the APRA's red carpet? Will a famous designer give you an outfit? Armani?"

Jane took her arm as they walked down the corridor. "Firstly, it's no red carpet for me. Remember what I said about keeping it low-key? I wouldn't even be going at all, but Amber said she would have more fun if I were there."

"I'm dying of cuteness! Dying! Call the campus ambulance!"

Jane laughed. She could always rely on her niece to bring the joy and enthusiasm. And today Jane had joy and enthusiasm of her own, which hadn't always been the case.

Her structured and safe life was tilting on its axis. She didn't know whether to hold on tight or let go.

CHAPTER 17

The promo director hired by the commercial TV station was a woman who seemed a few years younger than Amber. "That's great! Let's go for one more."

"Yep. Same starting mark?" she replied, thinking about how the Australian entertainment landscape seemed to change every time she returned. The change was slow—too slow—but noticeable. More women, more queer people, more people of colour. And the people with clout seemed to be getting younger. She smiled to herself. *Maybe I'm just getting older.*

It was nice, though. When she had been at the height of her fame, every event and every meeting had been packed with middle-aged white blokes. A roomful of them had yelled that she could kiss her career goodbye if she came out as lesbian.

She had gone from that meeting straight to a magazine interview. The cover story had been a modern reimagining of Ellen DeGeneres' *"Yep, I'm Gay"* photo shoot for Time magazine. It had been their best-selling issue in a decade.

"More smoke!" yelled the director.

The *Australian Idol* promo shoot was running behind schedule. Ratings had flagged in recent years, and the TV station had been contacting Amber's management for a while, offering to add her as a judge. The emails had gotten more insistent as the former female judge had quit for a better offer from *Britain's Got Talent.*

The money they were offering was ludicrously generous, but filming the contestant auditions segments and the live shoots would be gruelling. She wasn't precious about doing little promotional bits and bobs to keep herself in the public eye. She had never been a tortured artist that turned down any offers of money. But the time away from recording, touring, and generally being a musician had always been a deal breaker for her.

Now she had a reason to spend a big chunk of time back in Australia. She had a gorgeous flat in Sydney, overlooking Double Bay. A cousin had been living there rent-free for a long time, on the pretence of "looking after the place" for her. He didn't kick up any fuss about having to move out—surely he wanted to still be in the good books for when she moved back to the States, freeing up the flat again.

If I move back. She blinked up at the stage lights and shook her head. She really shouldn't get ahead of herself. Daydreams had been coming to her unbidden while she and Jane had been texting and calling each other from the opposite ends of the world. Jane loved the uni she worked at—maybe Amber could base herself there in Brisbane. They could buy a gorgeous old Queenslander house with a wraparound veranda. Get a dog, or one of those long-haired cats.

Get it together, girl! She was putting the cart a few kilometres before the horse, as usual. Just like with her former fiancée Alyssa Vixen, and the sculptor Marielle before her, for that matter. And Jane was sure to get spooked just like they had.

"OK, this is the take! It's been a long day; let's nail it," yelled the director.

The promo was not going to set the short-film world on fire anytime soon. They were the basic standard shots of her with the other judges. They were both well-preserved old pros who'd been doing this gig since the beginning of the franchise nearly two decades before. The three of them did slow motion poses for the camera. The one with a reputation for being mean had crossed his arms and scowled. Amber had been asked to smile and put her hand on her hip and garnered praise from the director about how well she did it.

"Low stakes and very low expectations," she had whispered to Teddy during a short break for a drink of water.

"You're on easy street now, darling," he replied. "Now, don't fuck this up for me. You can nail this shit without ever leaving third gear. And I'm looking forward to staying in the same place for the next few months. I want the chance to be a 'regular' at the bars on Oxford Street. The cute barman at The Gaslight Inn remembered my drink order last night."

"We've been here three days. How many times have you been to the bar?"

The shot they were doing now was for a teaser trailer. Amber, a silhouette shrouded in smoke-machine haze, would walk down the runway thing at the front of the famous *Idol* stage. But who was she? The teaser promo would bombard the airways and social media for a few days. Fake blind items reporting that the new judge might be other, less famous, big-haired, short women would be planted on forums and social media. Then the promo featuring non-silhouette Amber would drop, and there would be a frenzy of media ops and appearances.

"*Aaaaand,* action!"

She put one foot in front of the other, stopped at the end of the stage, and stood with a hip jutted.

"Cut! Amazing job, Amber. Really great work. You're a one-take wonder, babe."

Geez! This job so far had been like shooting fish in a barrel. Early in her career, she had needed to show real grit and a superhuman work ethic. And there had been no praise, no positive reinforcement or encouragement.

Maybe this *was* easy street. Hopefully it didn't make her soft. Or send her to sleep.

The shoot was running behind schedule because one of the judges, the other male one, not the "mean" one, had arrived late, taken too long in make-up, and had generally been a brat during the shoot.

Amber had thought she would be done before Jane arrived from the airport, so that she could meet her at the Double Bay flat. But when Jane had texted that her flight from Brisbane had landed, they had arranged for Jane to come to the set. They would still have a couple of hours to get ready for the APRA awards that evening.

Amber had originally offered to meet Jane at the airport, but Jane didn't want to deal with any fans that might decide to swarm. Amber had been upfront with her about the possibility. In LA, she enjoyed a relatively anonymous everyday life, but Australia was different. Any public outing could turn into a frenzy.

At the Channel 10 building for the shoot, and at the awards show tonight, there would be security staff tasked with keeping an eye on all the celebrities in attendance. But any impromptu outings to other locations would require a personal bodyguard arranged through her management agency.

Amber felt a twinge of sadness. A part of her wished that today she could have nothing on her schedule and she could go and pick up her…her what? Not girlfriend yet, or partner? She wished she could have quietly met Jane at the airport—no attention, no hiring of bodily protection staff, just them.

Did that mean she wished her whole career away? No, that wasn't right. She didn't. Her chest tightened when she thought about how much Jane hated the limelight, though. Nobody else she had dated had been such a private person. Some exes had downright loved the flash of a paparazzo's camera.

She swallowed and took a deep breath. She had been looking forward to seeing Jane again since the moment she had let her go at LAX. Three whole months ago! No point spoiling it now with pointless anxiety.

"That's a wrap on Amber. Thank you, darl. Sorry about all the delays."

"No worries. Great working with you. Thank you," she replied.

Amber sat on the edge of the stage and hopped down. Teddy was nowhere to be seen.

When he finally appeared, it was with someone tall at his shoulder. Amber held up her hand to shield her eyes from the bank of studio lights.

Jane.

Her heart jumped. Amber ran beyond the white lights and into the relative darkness and wrapped her arms around her. She looked up into Jane's smiling face, then pressed her mouth to hers.

She had built this moment up for weeks, had dreamt about it at night, but the reality was even better. Jane felt warm, solid, real. Her taste was familiar. Her smell comforting. Amber's knowledge of her seemed to stretch back years.

"Hi." Amber put the back of her hand to her own cheek, a little flustered by her big feelings.

"Hi," replied Jane. She smiled, took Amber's hand and pressed the knuckles to her lips. Her eyes seemed to acknowledge everything that was going inside Amber. "I missed you."

Amber smiled. The swirling storm in her chest stilled. She felt calm and happy. She stuck her fingers into the back of Jane's short hair, pulled her face down again and kissed her hard.

CHAPTER 18

Jane walked haltingly down the stepped aisle to the seat number on her phone screen. She was wearing a dark-green suit. Amber had mussed her hair all up and used some mousse stuff to make it look all over the place on purpose.

Jane had smiled at her reflection in the mirror and said the professors at work would fall off their chairs if she showed up to give a lecture like this.

Amber had given her a peck on the cheek and rearranged a wayward piece of hair. The nice make-up lady who had come to the flat smiled and said "aw", like it was the most natural thing in the world.

Jane was still taken aback when people accepted that she and Amber were dating. Her expected reaction was that they would do a double-take and rub their eyes with their fists, mouths hanging open, aghast and confused. "How could a beautiful woman like that choose to be with someone so ordinary and plain?" they would say.

However, the person at the front desk at Channel 10 studios and the make-up lady hadn't batted an eyelid. And Sara had been thrilled and excited but not surprised.

Jane bent to look at a row number (the auditorium was quite dark) and thought about how maybe people were less surprised by things than she'd thought they would be. Maybe the things Jane said and did were not so offensive and earth-shattering. The friendly counsellor she had been to after the break-up with Lauren had said it was not a fact that Jane had the ability to ruin any situation at any moment. It was just Jane's view of things.

She found her row, second from the front, and moved apologetically along to her seat. She probably should have recognised a lot of the people she was forcing to squeeze their knees sideways to let her though, but she couldn't have named a single one of them.

Amber's seat was vacant next to her. She had to perform near the start of the awards show and also present an award closer to the end, so she wouldn't be around much until later. She hadn't released any music in the past year and so wasn't up for any awards. She had told Jane she was happy about it—she had won so many over the years that she didn't like taking them away from up-and-coming acts.

Jane smiled. Amber was special. Her enthusiasm and kindness weren't just skin-deep. It went right down to the very middle, as far as Jane could tell.

She rubbed her palms on her thighs, reminding herself yet again that she didn't know Amber all that well yet. That was a fact, but Jane also had an illogical deeper suspicion that she knew Amber through and through.

Oop! Again she was overcome with the earth-tilting feeling. Maybe things could be true and not-true at the same time. She would never have entertained the notion a couple of months ago.

The stage lights came on, and everyone started clapping.

Two women came out wearing gowns, welcomed everyone, and told some jokes. It wasn't that different from a graduation ceremony at work, except that Jane's hair was messier and the women went on to introduce a musical act, who began playing a very thrashy song about buying expensive cars.

Jane tapped her foot to the rhythm. She was tone-deaf—no one note sounded different from any other. Her mother could be brought to tears listening to classical music, whereas Jane could tell where one note ended and another began, but that was pretty much it. Music with an interesting or driving beat was enjoyable to listen to, or sometimes very poetic lyrics could hold her attention. Other than that, music was background noise.

The hosts came back, followed by some other people giving out a couple of awards, and then there was a break, probably for the television broadcast to play some ads.

Jane looked around. There was a dark-haired man sitting next to her. "Look, our suits are nearly the same colour," she said to him. She held her sleeve next to his.

"So they are," he replied.

"I like how shiny and pointy your shoes are," Jane continued. "I should have gone to more effort."

"Thank you. Your ensemble is understated and classy. Not like me, always looking like I have something to prove."

"Oh, I don't think that's the impression you give at all. I flew in from Brisbane today. Where are you from?"

They chatted amiably until the lights went down and the hosts reappeared. Jane clapped loudly when they introduced the next performer—Amber.

She was wearing a gold dress with a short skirt, and she had shiny, gold make-up in streaks up her cheekbones. She shimmered under the lights.

Because she wasn't promoting any new music, she had decided to do a medley of all her "old hits". People in the crowd screamed when she launched into the first song, kind of a slower one about rain and floods. Then she grabbed an electric guitar off a stand and launched into a faster one about a heart to borrow. Then she put that down and sat at a grand piano and sang very loudly about "all my tomorrows". Jane could hear people singing along, looked around, and realised everyone she could see in the whole place was singing along, even Mr Shiny Shoes beside her.

The drums took over, very loud, and Amber ran to the front of the stage and ripped off the shirt of her dress. Now she was just in a gold leotard and gold high heels. Jane exhaled and ran the back of her hand across her forehead. Her collar felt very tight. Was she burning up?

The ad shoot had run late, so there hadn't been time that afternoon to have any moments alone together. They had made out until the nice make-up lady had arrived but hadn't had the opportunity to do anything more. Jane was suddenly very aware of the fact.

Amber belted out a lyric about "wanting to do things to you they don't teach in school" and pointed with an extended arm right at Jane. They locked eyes, and Amber gave her a wink before she turned away to go stand on the top of the piano and sing a song called "The Moonlight Moves Me."

Jane's whole body thrummed, like an electrical pulse was running through it. Amber had a power that was like magic. She was entrancing all the thousands of people in the crowd, and all that energy directed at her, even for just a moment, hit Jane so hard that she rocked back on her heels.

The audience all stood up. The people in front of Jane were dancing energetically, and when she looked up at the cheap seats above her, the balcony seemed to be heaving as everyone up there moved their bodies to the song.

Amber brought it all home by lifting up a spangled microphone stand over her head. As the song ended, the crowd roared. Amber held the pose and grinned, then threw her head back with a look of sheer joy, before blowing kisses and mouthing *thank you* to each section of the ecstatic audience.

Jane felt a pressure in her head, then realised she had tears in her eyes.

Amber was born to perform, and watching her so in her element, doing the thing she loved, had made Jane's chest ache. She cast her mind back over the last few years—had she felt like that doing her job, ever? When she'd first started as a researcher, getting into the flow of information, working with others, running ideas to the ground, and chasing capital-T "Truth", she had felt it. But not recently. Maybe when she got this associate professorship and had more autonomy to choose the projects she wanted, things would change.

As Amber moved offstage, Jane felt her absence like the sun setting. She wished she was waiting in the wings, ready to wrap her up in her arms. Why wasn't she?

When Jane first said she would go with her to the awards, Amber had bounced up and down with excitement. She had reminded Jane of Sara, whose enthusiasm Jane had always attributed to her youth. Now she knew some people bounced well into adulthood—maybe they bounced their whole lives. Jane didn't recall ever bouncing, even when she was Sara's age.

Amber had started rattling off how amazing the night would be—they would walk the red carpet together, do interviews with all the journalists and live streamers, and Amber could introduce her to some of her old friends from the biz. Jane had poured cold water all over it. Nicely—a splash here and a trickle there—but she had doused it completely nonetheless.

The university expects a certain image…certain promotion…associate professorship…distractions from my achievements…blah blah blah.

Jane winced now in the darkened auditorium. The importance of it all had paled beside the energy and love Amber had been able to whip up within the crowd with the moonlight song.

How important was any of her stuff? And why had she spent so many years of her life agonising over it all?

"We don't have many like her," said the dark-haired man as they took their seats again.

"No, she's very special," she replied. Her throat felt thick, and the tears threatened.

His forehead creased, and he patted Jane's arm. "Big music fan, hey?"

Jane nodded but did not speak. She was incapable of forming any words of explanation.

The hosts returned. One leant right up into the mic and yelled, "How about Amber Freaking Hatfield?! She's back, she's awesome, and she's just knocked our bloody socks off!"

The crowd clapped and whooped.

Two more awards were handed out. Jane clapped politely as a woman in an oversized T-shirt and baseball cap went up to receive a statuette, then a trio of young men in colourful sneakers.

Then the awards show took a break for more ads. People wearing black ran around on the stage moving instruments and microphone stands. A strange silence descended, which was quickly replaced with soft chatter from all parts of the crowd.

Someone a few rows back let out a "woo!". Jane turned and saw Amber walking down the aisle, holding the skirt of her silver, sparkly dress out to the side so she didn't fall down the wide, shallow steps. Some people who noticed her clapped as she walked by.

Amber acknowledged the recognition with smiles and nods. For a few people, she held out her outstretched arm in their direction and waved.

Everyone in their row had a smile and a kind word for her as they shifted to let her through.

She reached Jane and beamed. "Hi." She put her hand on Jane's arm and made a small motion to tilt her face up, like she was going to give her a kiss. She stopped herself, though and gave another tight-lipped smile.

"Hi," Jane replied. *Stupid, stupid, stupid.*

Amber was respecting Jane's boundaries and wishes. Nothing that would show the people here what they were to each other, what they did behind closed doors.

It was all wrong, though. Jane had big, tender feelings roiling around inside her. And she had to sit on her hands instead of throwing her arms around the amazing woman smiling up at her? She didn't deserve to be an associate professor, unless it was the position of Associate Professor of Dumb Idiots.

"Congratulations on an amazing performance," said Jane's new friend, the dark-haired man.

"You are too sweet. Thank you! It's been way too long since I've seen you. How did we let so many years go by?" Amber gave him a hug and a kiss on the cheek.

Jane scowled. *Nope, I never liked that man. Too chatty.*

"Time marches faster the older we get," he replied with a smile.

The house lights dimmed, and there was a shuffling sound as people resumed their seats.

"Have you enjoyed it so far?" Amber asked Jane as they settled in.

"It's been great. I loved your medley."

Amber grinned. "That makes me really happy." She looked up at the stage where the hosts were taking their places. She was still smiling.

As Jane watched her, the throat-aching feeling returned. Being around Amber was a roller-coaster of emotions—one minute she was full of joy at a great musical performance (which had never happened to her before) and the next she was going to blubber and have to ask her new friend (*enemy!*) for a hanky.

She looked over the dark-haired man.

He caught her eye, glanced at Amber, then back at Jane, then raised his eyebrows and nodded slowly. "I thought she was singing half those lyrics at you."

Jane didn't know what to say. She could feel her forehead creasing. She turned away.

Amber nodded towards him. "Did you introduce yourself?"

"We chatted," she said.

Amber's eyebrows shot up. "Wow."

Jane didn't think their interaction had deserved a *wow.* "I didn't catch his name, though. What is it?"

Amber made a half scoff, half-choking sound. "Nick. Nick Cave."

"Oh, I'll never remember that," Jane whispered. "Can you remind me if we see him again at cocktails?"

Amber's shoulders shook with silent laughter. "I'm happy to, if you're still struggling after he goes up to get his lifetime achievement award in a minute."

Jane glanced over at her neighbour.

He was suppressing a smile too.

Her face went warm.

He leaned sideways towards her and whispered. "Don't worry. I travel the world chasing anonymity. You've given me an unexpected gift tonight." He bowed his head briefly at her. "Now smile for the telly cameras when they point our way."

The hosts were talking again, and images of the dark-haired man glowering at the camera or screaming into microphones faded in and out on a big screen over the stage.

"Can we swap seats?" Jane asked Amber.

"Yep, sure," Amber whispered.

As Amber took her seat next to Nick Cave, Jane heard him mumble something.

"No, my friend's just a little camera shy."

Jane's skin burned. She was messing everything up. Amber was having a triumphant night, but she had to make lame excuses for Jane. *Maybe I'm foolish to think I can ever belong here.*

Amber leant against Jane and gave her arm a quick squeeze. Jane at once felt worse and better. Amber was so understanding, and Jane couldn't budge one centimetre on her resolution to protect her reputation. She clenched her fist. She couldn't change who she was and what she cared about. Maybe she should go before she did any more damage.

Everyone clapped, and the dark-haired man got up and went onto the stage.

Amber slid her fingers between Jane's and clasped her hand. "He was so chuffed you'd never heard of him once in your life," she said. Her eyes crinkled as she smiled again. "I'm so glad you're here with me, Jane. Thank you."

Jane squeezed her hand. The burning shame lessened. The thought of leaving had been physically painful, an instant hard ache in her chest. Jane made a new resolution: to do her best for this incredible woman. Tenderness welled up in her chest, and the throat-tightening returned.

Amber chuckled at something Nick Cave said in his speech.

Jane watched her lips curve and the fine lines around her eyes crease. She wanted to press soft kisses on that face, to whisper gentle things. Her chest was so full, she thought she might explode.

The crowd stood and clapped as Nick was handed a big statuette.

The hosts announced another short break.

Amber turned to her suddenly and quirked an eyebrow. She put her mouth to Jane's ear. "I'm not wearing any underwear," she whispered. "Do you want to get out of here?"

Amber's warm breath sent heat from Jane's ear all the way down her body. Amber's body brushed against Jane's—just a hint of pressure at her hip.

Her heart started to pound. "Yes, totally, yes. Let's blow this popsicle stand." It was something Sara always said. Jane had never said anything like it before.

Amber threw her head back and laughed, her eyes glinting with mischief and joy. She grabbed Jane's hand, and they made their apologetic but hurried way back down along their row.

CHAPTER 19

Amber thanked the Australian music gods that the APRA awards were always held in the same place. She knew the Sydney Town Hall well. Jane's hand was warm in hers. She held on tight, her burning need to hold onto Jane being channelled into this one grip. At least until they were behind closed doors.

She opened her dressing room door and pulled Jane inside. With a flourish, she pressed against Jane and reached to lock the door behind her.

Jane's face was flushed. Her skin was so pale that the redness showed in broad streaks down her cheeks when she was nervous. Or turned on.

Amber loved bringing her heat to the surface. She pushed Jane so that her back was against the wall next to the door.

Jane's eyes widened. "Wait, you mean here? Do it here?" she whispered.

"Yes," Amber whispered back. "What's the point of performing and having a swanky dressing room if you don't fuck in it?"

Jane blinked. Her lips parted.

Pressure pooled between Amber's legs. Jane's obvious struggle between good sense and physical desire was turning her on even more.

Jane was sexy as hell in a suit, but in that moment, Amber wanted to rip it off her and be skin to skin, able to satiate this burning desire.

Jane looked around the room, the streaks of pink extending down her neck. "But what if there are cameras?"

"In a woman's dressing room? That would be highly illegal."

The breath caught in Jane's throat.

Amber took pity on her. "Look, we don't have to. We can wait until we get back to the flat."

Jane exhaled with a faint groan. "No, I want you now." She pressed her mouth to Amber's neck and pulled her tightly against her body. She put her face close to Amber's.

Amber was about to kiss her mouth, but Jane pressed her fingers to Amber's lips. "Wait," she said.

Jane ran her hand up the inside of Amber's thigh, stopping just before she reached the top.

Amber's desire burned to an agonising level just above Jane's hand. She gasped.

"Are you really not wearing any undies?" Jane asked, her lips millimetres from Amber's.

"See for yourself," she said in a strangled whisper. She groaned as Jane moved her hand up, applying delicious pressure. She was slippery. Amber hadn't realised how wet she had become.

Jane moved her hand, sending pleasure radiating to all parts of Amber's body.

Amber needed to taste Jane. She moved to kiss her mouth again, but Jane ducked her head back with a playful smile. "Wait. Not much longer."

Jane increased her pressure the tiniest amount. Amber closed her eyes. All that existed for her right now was Jane's hand under her skirt—the movement and ecstasy of it. She bucked her hips, and her breathing quickly became a rhythmic pant. She had no control over the sounds she was making.

Jane kissed her hard.

Amber opened her mouth to the kiss and moaned loudly as Jane's taste and smell filled all her senses.

"I need you, I need you," Jane muttered with her face pressed against Amber's cheek. "Couch."

Amber maneuvered awkwardly backwards, her skirt still hitched up, but she did all she could to keep Jane touching her. At that moment, it was the most vital thing in the world.

Jane lay Amber back on the leather couch and kneeled in front of her. She slid the thin straps of Amber's dress down her shoulders, revealing her breasts.

As she took Amber's nipple in her mouth and licked, she pressed her fingers into her vagina.

"Oh God, yes. Please. Fuck, yes," Amber said, spreading her legs wide.

Jane plunged in one finger, then two.

Amber rocked her hips harder, pushing against Jane's hand, working the fingers in deeper and deeper. She held onto Jane's hair and gripped as the pleasure built and built.

Her orgasm hit her like a ten-tonne truck. She pulled Jane's face to hers with both hands and pressed her own face against it. Her body juddered uncontrollably. She gasped into Jane's ear.

Release and pleasure flooded her body as the shudders subsided.

She steered Jane by the shoulders so that she was sitting on the couch, and straddled her.

Amber's belly glowed warm as Jane's eyes roved over her breasts, still slick from moments before.

Jane's lips were parted, and her face was flushed in streaks that went right down her neck.

"I better not send you out there in this state," Amber said softly.

Jane looked up at her. "Hah! Not if you want me to be able to walk. I might do dirty dance moves on Nick Cave and get arrested."

Amber laughed and pressed her mouth to Jane's. She didn't remember sex with anyone else being as fun as this. She had loved how Jane had taken control, been deliberate, like every movement meant something. And now she wanted to make Jane feel good. She was tantalised by the thought. Anticipation got her all turned on again, just when she thought she had really reached her limit.

She kissed Jane's neck.

Jane threw her head back.

She undid Jane's tie and her shirt buttons, moving the shirt and jacket aside to reveal Jane's bra. She slid her hand down Jane's belly and undid her trousers button and zip.

She slid her tongue into Jane's mouth as she pushed her hand into Jane's undies, pressing against her clit with two fingers.

Jane groaned and moved against her hand with her hips while kissing Amber back hard.

Amber rocked her own hips up and down in time with Jane's. She worked her other hand around to Jane's back underneath her shirt and scrabbled blindly at the bra strap.

Jane broke their kiss to gasp, "It undoes at the front."

"Oh, thank fuck for that!"

Jane undid it for her.

Amber moaned as she cupped Jane's breast. She licked her own fingers, then ran their slickness over Jane's nipples.

Jane groaned and rocked her hips harder. She ran her hands up under Amber's skirt and grabbed her arse, pulling her frantically against her.

When Jane came, Amber felt it everywhere. Her pussy contracted around Amber's fingers, her rib cage bucked, and her hands clenched her bum. She wrapped her arms tightly around Amber and rested her head against her collarbone.

Amber sat sideways in her lap.

Jane moved her knees up so Amber was held tight in her arms and legs.

Amber rested her face against Jane's, then looked into her eyes. "You did that like you had something to prove," she said softly.

Jane took a deep breath and tilted her head to the side. "Maybe I do."

Amber kissed her, gently this time. There was more to say, but it didn't have to be tonight. Slow happiness moved through Amber like she was a loved-up lava lamp. She didn't need promises about tomorrow. Tonight was enough.

Thumping bass started up, and Amber lifted her head.

"Oh shit, that's the Something for Kate reunion. I've got to present an award after the next ad break. Will you help me with my dress?"

"Dress?" Jane brushed at the spangled fabric around Amber's middle. The skirt had ridden up again, and the top was still pulled down. "It's really more of a fancy belt at this stage."

Amber snorted with laughter.

Jane started to giggle too.

They stood up, started putting themselves back together.

Amber leant in and checked her make-up in the big mirror. Her happiness was written all over her face. A buzz that was also a warm kind of comfort filled her body.

Jane leant over next to her, grabbed a wipe, and started taking huge smudges of lipstick off her face, neck, and chest.

She caught Amber's eye in the mirror, and they both grinned again.

CHAPTER 20

Two days later, Amber sat in a bright-yellow armchair in the carpeted hallway of a Sydney commercial radio station.

Jane had flown back the day before for work.

Amber had put her hand up for some media schmoozing in Brisbane later in the week too, so she would see Jane again for a flying visit in a couple of days.

It had felt strange to wake up alone that morning. Which was strange in itself, since she had woken up alone every morning since the third of January, when Jane had left LA.

It was uncanny how, in a short time spent together, Jane could seep into all aspects of Amber's life. Like the two of them being together was the most natural thing in the world.

Teddy sat down on a bright-pink armchair beside her and handed her an iced oat latte.

"Thank you, you're an absolute angel," Amber said.

"I know," he replied, taking the lid off his double-shot mocha with extra chocolate. "Has the producer been out to see you?"

"Yep. Confirmed I'm on with Kayla, Bobby, and Hieu at 7:48."

Teddy winced. "Don't remind me of how early in the morning it is right now. Did we really need to do this at the crack of sparrow's fart?"

Amber snorted. "The station reps said it's got to be the younger drive-time audience. Gen X are going to watch *Idol* this season or not—nothing we can do to influence them. But me being announced as judge might cut through with millennials. Something about childhood nostalgia."

Teddy raised an eyebrow. "And I'm not allowed to tell you you're old? The reps can get away with telling you grown-arse adults are making decisions because they remember you back when they were teeny-tiny children."

Amber scoffed and rolled her eyes. "You can't rankle me, Ted. I'm finally dating one of these grown-arse adults you're talking about. Remember Alyssa tried to convince me to change my birth date on Wikipedia so that people would think I was three years younger?"

"I remember Alyssa and Marielle and Shauna and Lachlan. Ash and Calliope were before my time, but I can get a sense of them based on what came after."

"Haha. Yes, I have quite a few burning piles of wreckage in my romantic past. Thanks for the reminder."

He crossed his legs and sniffed his coffee. "You're welcome, babes. Any time." He moved his cup to his lips but lowered it again without taking a sip. "Dating, huh?"

"You've lost me."

"That's what you and Professor Sexy are doing?"

"Yessssss. We're arranging to meet at certain times, then getting together with romantic intentions at those set times. Why? How would you classify it?"

Teddy pursed his lips and looked at the ceiling. "Me? No, you're right. You've just correctly stated how Webster's Dictionary defines dating. Nothing to add." His eyes darted from one part of the hallway ceiling to another.

Amber narrowed her eyes at him. She waited.

"Fine!" He sat up straight. "You know I don't like getting involved."

"True. My relationships usually fall apart without any help from you."

"Exactly. Now, The Professor is great. One really good thing is that there's no chance she's stringing you along to get extra social media followers."

"Uh, yah," Amber scoffed. "She only has LinkedIn, and that's because the uni made it a rule in the staff handbook."

"Yes, and that's a good thing. Remember Shauna asked for birthday presents from sponsors that year and made you give them to her on a live stream?"

"How could I forget?"

"Jane's, like, the opposite of that energy. Which is good. I'm not commenting, but I'm going to ask you a question. Is that OK?"

"Is 'is that OK' the question? If so, the jury's out."

His look was withering. "Don't try your aunt jokes in the studio with the young people listening, 'kay? Now, do you think that maybe Jane, you know, swings too much the other way?"

Amber knit her eyebrows. "I know sexuality's a spectrum, but I don't think Jane's going to dump me for a dude anytime soon."

He tsked and waved his hand to dismiss her comment. "No, geez. I mean, does she think being a popstar, you know, your life's work, is icky?"

"Icky?"

"Like, yuk?"

A door to their left burst open, making them both jump.

The producer approached. "We've thrown to an ad break, Amber. They're ready for you in the studio."

"Thanks." She stood and held up her oat latte. "Is it OK if I bring this?"

"No worries, as long as you don't spill it on the equipment."

A mental image of her doing just that, sparks flying everywhere, ran through her head.

Teddy wordlessly took the cup from her hand as she followed the producer.

Amber looked over her shoulder at him, and he gave a reassuring thumbs up.

It was like he could read her mind sometimes.

"Amber!"

Three dazzling smiles beamed at her from the other side of a thick glass window.

"Oh, hi," she replied. "Sorry, can you hear me in there?"

"Yep, absolutely," said the one called Kayla. "They put the glass up during COVID and decided to keep it. Everyone's getting way less colds. A lot of celebs come here straight off international flights, so the infection risk is high."

"Right, of course. Sorry. I've been in the States too long, I guess. Less of this stuff goes on over there." She waved both hands at the glass, the bottles of hand sanitiser, and the producer going at a big set of headphones with an antibacterial wipe.

All three radio hosts laughed.

Amber chuckled also.

"Have a seat," said the producer. The hosts sat down in front of big microphones on the other side of the glass.

"We're here, as promised, with songstress superstar and local legend Amber Hatfield!"

"Thank you so much for having me."

"I am so excited you're here," Kayla said. "I have to tell you something. It's a bit of a humble-brag, but I won my school's talent contest in Year 5 with a rendition of "The Moonlight Moves Me". I gave very specific costuming instructions to my mum."

Amber laughed. "Oh my goodness, how precious. Let me guess—star diamonds next to your eyes?"

The hosts all clapped and laughed. "Yes!" Kayla said. "Everything just like the film clip."

"Well, congratulations to ten-year-old you. I'm honoured to have been your muse."

Amber felt the old interview muscles kicking in. This was like riding a bike. The last few years in the States hadn't brought as many mainstream media interviews—there had been a few podcasts, and she left it mostly up to Teddy and her reps to decide what she should say in any planned social media posts. But she had done countless radio interviews in her teens and twenties. It was an equation: be down-to-earth and funny and sell the product.

"You're back in town at the moment, Amber," another host said. "Now, rumours have been absolutely swirling. Is it a new album, tour, fragrance—or did you just miss proper coffee over there in the US?"

Geez, these young hosts were pros! She didn't even have to sell the product herself today.

"It's none of those things actually, Hieu. I can officially announce, I've got permission, I swear, that I am…joining *Australian Idol* as a judge for the upcoming season, premiering this month!"

The hosts all cheered. Kayla said, "Oh my God!".

Amber shot her a smile. The station would have told these three in advance, but they were sweet to add some drama to the moment.

"It's been a few years since you've been back. What's it like being home again?"

"It's been so amazing. I was lucky enough to go to the APRAs with—" She stopped short. "With, um, with Nick Cave getting the lifetime achievement award."

"Love Nick Cave."

"Love that guy!"

"Yes," Amber continued. "And, well, just bumming around the old haunts, you know. Drinking great coffee, like you said." She reached for her latte, then remembered that Teddy had it.

The three faces on the other side of the glass watched her, maybe waiting for her to fix her answer to something less lame, or at least something they could tie back into the *Idol* conversation to make the TV station happy.

Amber blinked a few times. *Jane.* She had wanted to tell them she had spent time with Jane, gone to the awards, that Jane was going to join her in Melbourne because she had booked a performance there.

She was usually open with the people she interacted with. Sure, she didn't tell every radio DJ everything about her life, but she enjoyed the natural flow of energy and conversation, even in these official paid chats designed as content for an audience.

Now it was like the glass wall between her and these three nice, professional up-and-comers in the entertainment industry was an actual barrier. She had to guard what was foremost in her mind, block the natural flow. She felt like a fish trying to breathe air.

"And, well, yeah, of course I've been tapping back into the local music scene. There are so many new acts to be excited about. And with *Idol,* we hope to uncover even more. The endgame is to give our fabulous Aussie singers a platform and a sustainable entertainment career that might not otherwise be available to them."

OK. Her bike had wobbled, but she was back on track now.

She finished the interview on autopilot. When they played a song ("The Moonlight Moves Me", in honour of Kayla's talent show triumph), she thanked the hosts and waved goodbye through the glass.

Out in the hallway, Teddy had a smile plastered onto his face. It was maybe a little too broad. "You did great, babes!" he said. The smile dropped a couple of watts. "I didn't get in your head about The Professor, did I?"

"No, not at all. I would be thinking about her either way. Was that little stumble so obvious?"

They set off down the hallway towards the studio entrance.

"No, of course not! I only clocked it because I thought for a millisecond you were going to go official with the relationship live on national radio. I didn't think The Professor had signed off on publication."

"Noooo, she definitely has not." Amber sighed and took back her coffee. "I think I'm just in my head. Long-distance messes with your mind. I mean, I know you know my relationship patterns."

"Uh, yeah. You try to decipher what the other person wants, then tie yourself up in knots trying to be that thing."

"Wow, quick with the answer there, Dr Freud." She gave him a tight-lipped smile. "You're right about this whole thing being on Jane's terms. But it really is temporary. The job interview is this week. And whether she gets the job or not, everything changes. The stakes disappear."

"I guess we'll know for sure in a few days."

"Exactly. I really hope her, well, 'distaste' of the public-facing part of my job—like you were talking about—I hope that can fade to a background hum rather than be front and centre every time we go through the front door."

"The yuk."

"Such a way with words! Yes, the yuk."

"I hope so too, babes. And I hope once her big interview is done that you're going to start asking for what you want. This thing is never going to look the way you want if you don't ask for it. The Professor might be smart up here"—he pointed to his cranium like he was the Scarecrow in *The Wizard of Oz*—"but she doesn't seem so smart about other stuff."

Amber looped her arm into his. She had talked herself into feeling brighter. This situation with the absolute secrecy was not forever. The end was in sight.

"She's smart in all the ways that matter, if ya know what I mean?" She winked and put her finger to the side of her nose. "In the sheets."

Teddy screwed up his face. "Geez, Amber. Inappropriate much? My ears are delicate flowers!"

She laughed as they approached the security desk to sign out. She had told Teddy her hopes, and that would surely help manifest them.

CHAPTER 21

Jane threw her speaking notes onto the lectern beside her and strode forwards to the edge of the raised speaking platform. Row upon row of faces were arrayed before her, reaching well above her head in the packed lecture theatre.

"There are no absolutes in the interactionist perspective of sociology," she said. "A person is not one fixed thing. We are millions and millions of versions of ourselves, depending on who or what we are interacting with. Let me give you an example: Right now, I'm here, up the front, with the room's mics pointed at me, telling you things. In this interaction, I'm meant to assume you don't know or understand anything I'm talking about."

"I don't," a teenage boy in the fourth row called out, receiving a handful of tittered laughs.

"It's all in the assigned reading, Brandon. You might want to check it out sometime." Jane got the bigger laugh. "Our behaviour for the two-hour timeslot for this Friday evening lecture—which I'm aware overlaps with happy hour at Redroom, so I appreciate your attendance." Jane paused for another laugh. "Our behaviour here is not governed by our innate personalities, impulses, or even our morals. We're completing an interaction, and we're all playing by the rules and expectations of this interaction. Well, except perhaps Brandon."

Brandon raised both hands and nodded and grinned at his fellow students, turning all the way around to acknowledge the laughter from those in the nosebleed seats.

Jane smiled. "Can anyone else tell me an interaction where the rules mean you behave a certain way?"

Brandon raised his hand. "On a date with a cutie."

Jane nodded. "Great example. The rules of romantic interactions are complex. You do things in these settings that you never do out in the world in other everyday situations. At least, I very much hope so."

Another polite laugh, but the energy was flagging a few percentage points. Jane glanced at her phone on the lectern. "All right, we'll leave it there. We can pick up on the interactions of romance next week." She raised her voice over the general shuffle of tablets and laptops being put into bags. "For now, I'll just make sure you know the most important aspect of the rules of dating. Let's hear it from resident love expert, Brandon. What's the most important thing? Give me the C-word."

He opened his mouth to shout a reply.

Jane held up an index finger. "Nope, the other C-word."

"Consent," Brandon said, then stood and bowed to applause and a few cheers.

"Enjoy your Friday night, everyone. See you next week."

Students walking across the front of the theatre on their way out thanked her and wished her a good weekend.

She put her printed notes in her bag and packed up her laptop, sighing as quiet descended and the energy in the room departed with the students. Some remnants of that energy still thrummed through her. *A job well done.* It was always a win when she could pull of the five-to seven p.m. Friday lecture, where the students' concentration threatened to wander off at any moment.

Tonight was even sweeter because Amber was flying in at that moment, and she could pick her up at the hotel on her way home.

Jane grinned and hurried to pack her belongings away.

Footsteps echoed.

Jane looked up, surprised the sound was approaching down the lecture hall steps, rather than heading for the door and the campus bar a few buildings over.

A slight figure with a ponytail draped over her shoulder and a baseball cap pulled down low over her eyes reached the bottom of the stairs.

Jane was shocked with recognition a moment before the person pulled off the baseball cap with a flourish and tossed it to one side.

"Surprise," Amber said, palms spread wide.

Jane's eyebrows shot up. Happiness welled up in her chest, and she grinned, but the feeling was tamped down by a stab of anxiety. She roved her gaze once around the big hall. Nobody else there. "I'm meant to collect you at the hotel later."

"I know. Teddy and I got to the airport laughably early. I was looking forward to seeing you, you know. So we were in the Qantas lounge, and they came up and tell us there are seats available in First on an earlier flight. So here I am. Is that OK?" Amber quit her "big reveal" pose, and a crease appeared between her eyes.

Jane opened her mouth and closed it again. *Was this OK?* It was unexpected, and she was caught off guard. But seeing Amber here in front of her set the molten-gold feelings swishing around inside her again. *What was the harm?* "Of course it's OK. It was surprising to see you out of the blue. But good."

Amber's exhaled and dropped her shoulders. "I didn't want to wait." She was wearing the yellow T-shirt she had worn to Bill and Barbara's house the day before New Year's Eve. The one that clung in all the right places.

Jane's breath got stuck in her throat and she coughed. She didn't make a conscious decision, but her arms motioned forward to hold Amber tight. Before she could do more than twitch, a door banged open and a student bustled in.

"Oh, hi. Sorry, Jane. I think I dropped my phone next to my seat." A student descended the stairs two at a time. "I think I was here?"

Jane looked down at the floor to give herself a moment to recover from the shock of near discovery. "Don't apologise, Cassidy. You were sitting in the sixth row, I believe."

"Yep, nice! Here it is. Awesome. Bye. Have a great weekend." She slung her backpack over her shoulder and waved as she reached the end of the row. "Hold up." She stopped short and wheeled around. She narrowed her eyes and pressed her lips together so tight, her mouth disappeared. "Are you...Amber Hatfield?"

Amber shot a look sideways at Jane.

Jane could only give the minutest of shrugs. *No point in denying.*

"Yes, I am."

"Wow! You're all over TikTok because of the *Idol* announcement." Cassidy descended a couple of stairs. "I saw your *Raise the Roof* tour at Boondall. I was obsessed."

"Aww, thank you. I remember it well. 2012. How old were you?"

"I was eight, I think. Oh my God! Can I get a photo with you? My cousin Gretchen is going to flip."

Amber hesitated. She didn't look at Jane, but the tension in Amber's neck made it seem like she wanted to.

Jane leant sideways against the lectern. *Talk about the interactionist perspective!* Time spent with Amber so often took sharp turns when she was forced to step into her "beloved popstar" persona.

Right now, the stakes were low. Jane's heart rate had steadied after the fright of Cassidy bursting in, nearly catching her lecturer in a compromising position. Now there was nothing to do but watch the interaction play out.

Amber ascended the stairs and took Cassidy's proffered phone. "Wow! You're tall. I'm going to stand up here on this step so we can be the same height."

Cassidy's delighted giggle reverberated around the hall. It was the laugh of someone who was eight years old again.

Jane supressed a smile.

After they took the selfie, Cassidy threw her arms around Amber and thanked her profusely. She ascended a couple of steps, then whirled around again. "Hey, wait. What are you doing here?" she asked.

"I...uh, uhh," Amber stuttered.

Jane had a stab of conscience. Amber hated lying. "She's looking for her niece, but came to the wrong building," Jane said. "Her niece is studying..." Her mind went blank. *Should it be something that sounds like sociology? Scientology? No!*

"Molecular biology," Amber said.

"Oh, you're way off," Cassidy said. "The labs are *waaaaay* over the other side."

"Yes! Um, ma'am— " Jane addressed Amber, wincing but recovering quickly. "I can escort you to the labs, if you would like?"

Amber, her back to Cassidy, puffed her cheeks out, fighting a laugh. "Why, how delightful!" With a huge grin, she turned back to Cassidy. "And they say chivalry is dead."

Cassidy furrowed her brow. "Well, it was nice meeting you. Bye, Jane." She took off, the door shutting behind her.

Amber approached Jane. "She must have realised happy hour was nearly done. Hey, I really enjoyed watching you, you know, do your thang.

I don't have as much control of my audience every set. You had them in the palm of your hand."

Jane's face went hot. "Thank you. It really means a lot to hear you say that. Young people are going to save us all. You know, this year I put in my lecturer bio about my autism, and the students didn't bat an eyelid. Some of them have approached me, and we've had wonderful discussions about their own neurodivergence.

"The uni wanted me to keep it a big secret, but you have to give kids more credit. I love teaching. When it's good, it's the best."

"Well, I think your students can tell you love it. Now, shall we away, noble escort? To the labs?"

Jane chuckled. "To the labs, milady."

Amber crammed her hat back on, pulling the brim so far down, she had to tilt her head back to see where she was going.

Jane opened her mouth to tell her not to worry about it but stopped herself. It would be less than ideal if any faculty member saw Amber getting into Jane's car. *Less than a week until the job interview. Then some of this madness can stop.*

They made it to the safety of the car interior without being discovered. Jane fumbled with the keys. It was so quiet and still in the intimate space that she could hear Amber's breathing. She was desperate to kiss her, but there was still a tiny chance someone might see.

Amber didn't make any move to initiate contact either.

As Jane drove, they chatted about the *Idol* publicity, Jane's upcoming job interview, and Teddy's exploits at the Oxford Street bars and pubs. It was easy, like talking on the phone with her, but desire was building up inside Jane like a volcano about to blow. *That damn yellow T-shirt isn't helping.*

In Jane's townhouse, with the door shut behind them, Jane flicked on the hallway light. She squinted against the brightness after the dark outside but was glad to be able to look at Amber properly. Jane could tell she was tired from travelling—the crow's feet were a little more prominent, and there were hints of dark shadows under her eyes, but only if you got up close enough to be able to see them.

Jane got close enough, and fierce gratitude burned through her. She put her hand to Amber's face and ran a gentle thumb over her smile lines.

Amber's lips parted.

Jane kissed her and pulled her close. She tried to make up for all the many times she should have kissed and held Amber out in the world since they had met. She gripped her waist, and Amber's stomach let out a ravenous grumble.

They both smiled.

"Sorry," Amber said. "I haven't eaten since Sydney."

"Don't apologise. What kind of host am I? I haven't even offered you water. Just accosted you half a meter inside the front door."

Amber pressed her lips to Jane's cheek. "Don't you apologise. Accost me until the cows come home if you make it feel that good."

"Let's order some food. I've been so busy with work, there's absolutely nothing in the house."

Later, when they were sitting on the couch with full bellies, Jane put her arm around Amber.

Amber snaked her arm across Jane's belly and rested her head against Jane's chest.

Could this be my life all the time? A forceful longing for the possibility took hold of her. But it was soon squashed down and chased away by fear. Things as perfect as Amber didn't happen to people like Jane.

"Your heart's going a mile a minute," Amber said. She looked up, tender concern written all over her face.

Jane searched her eyes. Safety, affection—all the feelings coursing through Jane were reflected back. The evidence in front of her pointed to the conclusion that Amber felt the same way about her. But people had a habit of twisting and slipping through Jane's fingers. There was no way to predict or prevent it. Her fear whispered that this was better evidence—based on proven history and not unpredictable, quicksilver emotions.

"I–I'm sorry. I'm in my head a little bit," Jane said. Her heart started to pound uncomfortably, and pressure built up in her throat and behind her eyes.

"Hey now. Shhh-sh-shh." Amber ran her hand through Jane's hair. "Don't worry. You're OK. You know what we can do?"

Jane shook her head.

"We can pull down our glass dome. Remember? Here." She reached up and pulled the imaginary dome down over the both of them. "Better?"

Jane nodded, not trusting herself to talk yet.

Amber rested her head against Jane's chest again and put both arms around her.

The dome was helping. Jane focused on Amber's body against hers. Nothing else, for now.

The panic receded.

"There," Amber said as Jane's heartbeat slowed to a normal human rhythm.

They sat for a bit, just hugging and breathing. Jane ran her hand down Amber's back. "I remember this shirt. You were wearing it when you came to Barbara and Bill's." The words were little more than a murmur because Jane didn't want to move her chin from where it was pressed into Amber's hair.

"The day I met Selena Gomez. Of course. How funny you remember what I was wearing. You usually don't clock outfits."

"You're right. I have a specific memory of this one, though. You were looking out the living room window, and I noticed, well, you wear this shirt well. Extremely well. It clings in all the right places."

Amber's hand clenched into a fist, taking hold of Jane's work shirt. "Oh. How very interesting." She sat up, a glint in her eye. "Are you *sure* this is the same one?" She reached up under the back of the shirt and undid her bra, pulling it out below her left armpit and dropping it to the floor.

Jane's breathing grew heavy as her eyes roved over the shape of Amber's breasts under the thin, soft fabric. "Well." Her voice came out as a rasp, and she cleared her throat. "It's very important we get to the bottom of this. I'll need to investigate further." She pressed her lips to Amber's jawline, then breathed on her neck, teasing the sensitive skin there with her tongue.

Amber groaned and threw her head back.

Jane ran her thumb with agonising slowness over Amber's nipple. It hardened at her touch.

Desire thudded in Jane's body. She pressed Amber against the couch and took her nipple, fabric and all, in her mouth.

Amber gasped and gripped Jane's back with both hands.

Jane looked up, resting her chin on Amber's stomach. "I'm getting your T-shirt all wet. Is that okay?"

Amber laughed and wrapped her legs around Jane's hips. "I can wash the shirt, Jane. I'll burn the damn shirt! Just keep going."

Jane grinned and did what she was told.

CHAPTER 22

"Could you get a more perfect morning than this?" Amber asked the next day as they walked into a park with giant dark-green fig trees. She and Jane had eaten Weet-Bix at home, then decided to walk down together to a nearby café and get coffee.

Amber wore a large, wide-brimmed straw hat and even bigger sunglasses than the day before.

"Brisbane in autumn is pretty special," Jane agreed. "The café's just around the corner. We can come back here and drink our coffees, if you like."

"Perfect." Amber caught hold of Jane's hand and meandered onto the grass towards the big river. A catamaran-style ferry went past at speed. Even though the river was brown, the little waves caused by the boat sparkled gold in the sun. The sky was a perfect cornflower blue overhead. Amber slid her sunglasses down her nose. "What's the picture on the ferry?"

"Oh, the boats are usually called CityCats, but two of them are done up to be CityDogs for the kids TV show *Bluey*. It's set in Brisbane. That one's Bluey, and there's another one for her sister, Bingo."

Amber grinned. "That's whimsical as hell, and I love it. Your city's cute, you know that?"

"You're pretty cute yourself," Jane said and pressed a soft kiss to Amber's lips.

Amber's chest fluttered. She tilted her head back, holding on to the top of her sunhat to keep it from falling off. Her eyes lingered on Jane's after the kiss, the flutter becoming a thump at the tenderness she saw reflected there. "I could look at your face all day."

Jane let go of her. "All the wrinkles and sags, you mean?" She rubbed her nose.

"You're not the best at taking a compliment. In my biz, we say if you've got it, flaunt it."

Jane took her hand again and looked out at the river. "That's what Barbara says to me. The compliment bit, not the showbiz bit. She says my last relationship undermined my confidence."

"Lauren." Amber pursed her mouth. "I think this is the first time I've ever disliked someone I've never met." She squeezed Jane's hand. "If I ask you something, you don't need to answer, OK?"

"Shoot."

"You were with Lauren for ages. I've got a negative impression of her, to say the least. So I guess I'm wondering why..."

"Why did I stay with her for fifteen years?"

"Yeah." Amber held her shoulders rigid. Part of her wanted to hit "undo" and go back to the pleasant walk without awkwardness or discomfort. Amber stared at Jane's face as she waited for her to answer.

"It didn't start out bad." Jane looked out towards a JetSki bumping along the Brisbane River. "At first, it felt like exactly where I was meant to be. Barbara's older than me, and I had looked at her and Bill as the example of the perfect marriage. They actually enjoy spending time together. They flirt with each other when they're at dinner parties." She scoffed with a smile. "When I realised I was gay, my family was really supportive, but I still, I suppose, didn't have a real-life example of a lesbian relationship as solid as theirs. I dated a few women, but I could never seem to make the jump from casual to serious. I never understood why.

"Then I met Lauren, and she wanted to be my girlfriend right away. It was like she was fascinated with every aspect of my life. In hindsight, it bordered on controlling, but at the time, it seemed like she cared. It seemed like love. We had some good times too. All fifteen years weren't a nightmare.

"I don't know. Everyone's got good and bad. Lauren is flawed, and for a long time I think she based her self-esteem on being part of the academic power couple that was us. She built me up as long as we were creating this picture of a perfect life together." She shrugged. "Sometimes I want to write the whole relationship off, as if it were one big con. Brush myself off and move on."

Amber wandered a few steps and leaned against a low stone wall. "It's not that simple though, is it? It's like if you write that person off completely, make them nothing, you lose something of yourself as well."

Jane's nodded, thoughful. "That's exactly right. That's what I've been struggling with." She opened her mouth as if to say more but closed it again. Side-by-side, they watched the water lapping gently around some mangrove plants below them.

Amber closed her eyes for a moment. The sun warmed her, and a gentle breeze played across her skin. Jane's arm rested against hers, comfortable and solid. "I struggle too. My mum is a full-blown narcissist. She saw me—well, probably still sees me—as an extension of herself. Which was fine when I was little. But when I grew up, it was like she only saw what I brought in for us—money and respect, security she had never had when she was growing up.

"She didn't see *me* at all. And if *she* didn't see me, and she was the person I loved most in the world, what did that mean? I was lost." Tears spilled hot down her cheeks.

Jane gently took the big sunhat from Amber's head and wrapped her arms around her.

Amber pressed her face against Jane's T-shirt. Jane's chin rested against the top of her head.

Amber breathed, focusing on being held. Being safe. "A lot went down. I've don't have any relationship with her at all anymore." Her voice was steady. "But I get what you mean. She's not bad all the way through. We would dance to Kylie Minogue before bed when I was a kid. I'm not ready to let her back in, but I'm working towards something for myself. Forgiveness isn't quite the right word."

"Words are overrated sometimes."

Amber took a few more deep breaths against Jane's chest. The old deep panic and frustration that sometimes rose up in her—had done ever since she could remember—ebbed away. "That coffee is calling to me. We'd better—" She burst out laughing when she saw Jane.

"What?"

Jane was wearing Amber's big straw hat over her own baseball cap. She looked up. "Oh. Yes. Well, it's a nice hat. I didn't want to dirty it by dropping it on the ground." She put the hat back on Amber's head.

"You're sweet. It's just, the mental image of you embracing a weeping woman, standing there wearing two hats—it got me." She wiped her cheeks dry.

Jane grinned and took her hand as they headed towards the café. "I'll give you a two-hat hug anytime you like."

They stepped into the deep, muggy shade of a Moreton Bay fig tree, but Amber was still warm as if she carried the golden sunlight with her. "I'll take you up on that."

CHAPTER 23

Jane finished her sandwich and put her little lunch box back into her desk drawer. She always had the same thing on her midday break—Vegemite on wholemeal bread and an apple for dessert. Her father had eaten the same lunch every day he worked at the university until his retirement five years before. He had taken only six sick days in his entire time there.

Jane smiled as she thought of him. One of his long-time colleagues from the biotechnology department would be on the panel for her interview today. It was protocol to have a senior representative of another area of the uni be part of the decision-making. Dr Hossein had written on his conflict of interest form for the interview process that he had gone out for customary "wet the head" drinks with Jane's dad to celebrate Jane's birth and had been present at her first birthday party.

She glanced at the clock. More than an hour until the interview. It was a very long time to eat an apple. Too long.

She checked her phone. No new messages, but she tapped the icon to see the string of texts Amber had sent her that morning, wishing her good luck and light-filled energy and saying she would be thinking of her. Amber had said on the phone the night before that she would be in meetings with her management team until the afternoon, so no chance of a call or text chain now.

It had been hard to say goodbye to Amber after her visit a few days before. Ridiculously, it had felt nearly as hard as saying goodbye in LA, even though they had a date set in a couple of weeks' time to meet up again. The more time she spent with Amber—and the more her feelings deepened—the harder it got to be away from her.

Jane put her hands to her cheeks and exhaled.

She closed her lunch box drawer and stood, brushing off some sandwich crumbs. She would go for a walk, burn off some nervous tension, then eat her apple just before the interview so her blood sugar would be nice and high. She nodded once as she strode down the corridor.

The day was overcast and a little cool, not enough to need a jumper but much more comfortable for a midday stroll than summer would have been. She walked under the porticos of an old sandstone building, the marble floor echoing with her footsteps and those of dozens of students on their way to and from classes. Across a large lawn edged with palm trees was the super-modern glass and steel creative arts building.

Jane walked at a good pace down a green slope to a series of ponds the uni tried to call "lakes". Fig trees created large areas of welcome shade. This would have to be a shorter walk than normal, or else she would turn up for her interview shiny and smelling of sweat.

A colourful guinea fowl made a diagonal run towards her from the water's edge. It was a big bird, coming up to above her knee, and it made a big fuss by flapping its stubby wings and making a honking cry.

Jane looked over her shoulder at him and kept walking. "Calm down, you. There's no point either of us getting worked up. I have no interest in making that murky dam my territory." He honked once more and watched her walk off, puffing his chest as if in victory.

Jane slowed as she reached the creative arts building again. The climb from the ponds hadn't been strenuous, but she didn't want to risk her unruffled visage.

"Jane!" a voice called from across the lawn.

Jane didn't have to look up to see who it was. Her stomach sank.

Lauren raised her arm and waved as she walked towards Jane with purpose. She was smiling as she reached her, as if this chance meeting would bring pleasure to the both of them. Jane just hoped she could extricate herself, unruffled visage intact.

"I saw you head down to the lakes and thought you would be back soon. I wanted to wish you the absolute best for your interview today."

Not a chance meeting, then, Jane thought. "Thank you." She wanted enough time to eat her apple and gather her thoughts before she had to go in. "I had better check I'm fully prepared," she said, setting off again towards her office.

Lauren fell in step beside her.

Jane sighed inwardly. She remained silent, waiting to see what Lauren had to say, since she had decided to tag along on this journey.

"I hear dear old Dr Hossein is on the panel. Kenneth and Terrence were talking about it in the staffroom the other day, saying they had heard he was an old chum of your dad's. I told them I was sure the proper procedures had been followed to avoid any perceived conflict of interest. Don't worry."

Jane shot her a glance. *Don't worry?!* She didn't have a thing to worry about a few seconds ago before Lauren had mentioned those two gossip-obsessed fossils. Both Kenneth and Terrence had applied for the associate professorship but had not gotten an interview.

Lauren's silence indicated she was waiting for a response.

"Thank you," said Jane.

"You know, Jane, I really believe your dad will be proud of you whether you get the job or not. You're the youngest in the pool to get an interview, and not much older than he was when he was made associate professor."

"Thank you." It was really becoming ludicrous how many times she had had to thank Lauren in the last couple of minutes. She felt like one of those stuffed teddy bears that had a catchphrase every time you pressed its stomach. *Thank you. For wasting my interview preparation time. Thank you!*

"Jane," she placed her hand on Jane's arm and stopped walking.

Jane slowed to a stop too, reluctantly, like an eighteen-wheel freightliner on a wet highway. She opened her mouth to make a quick apology so she could hurry off.

"I'm glad I've got this chance to speak to you before you go in there," Lauren said. "I know you're well aware, but this position is a cut above. They're going to give it to someone they can put on brochures to advertise the university all over the world. Someone who will attract the biggest names in academia to the international symposia. Enhance the institution's reputation. It's much more of a commitment than a lecturer's level of employment, and I've seen the role take over people's lives."

The back of Jane's neck prickled. The seconds passed heavily, in slow motion. The sand had gone clumpy and wasn't going through the hourglass right.

Lauren glanced left, then right, and continued in a lowered voice. "People have been noticing that you're not quite as, how to put this, committed, conscientious, as usual."

Jane bit down on a sudden urge to laugh out loud. The prickling stopped. She thought about what Amber's reaction would be when she Facetimed her later. She would gasp and laugh. *In what order? Maybe both at the same time.*

"Really? What did they base this judgement on?" Jane managed to keep her tone neutral.

Lauren blinked a few times. "Well, you have been leaving earlier in the evening. And you took Friday off, for a trip away, less than two weeks before this interview."

Jane pressed her lips together, hoping the smirk wouldn't show. She wanted more ridiculousness from Lauren to tell Amber. The mental image of the whole faculty craning their necks at the staffroom window to watch her walk to her car at the end of a long day, then murmuring together about how early it was, nearly made her lose it. Old Kenneth and Terrence looking at the leave roster and exclaiming about her taking one day off, surmising that it must be for a frivolous trip away, was delightfully ludicrous. In truth, she had so much leave built up that the dean had begged her to take more time off in case HR came knocking.

Two spots of red appeared on Lauren's cheeks. "I felt it was important to let you know. To help. In the interview, well, I thought it would be useful for you to know what impression the panel might have formed, so you can counteract it. Get on the front foot." She looked at the ground as she ran out of things to say.

Jane looked at her properly for the first time since they had started talking. This woman, fastidiously dressed, hair so straight and uniform it barely moved in the breeze, had once loomed so large in her life that she couldn't see anything else.

But Lauren was small. She lived in a fantasy land where she exercised power over the chess pieces in her life with lies and petty power plays.

An ache started up in her throat that took her inward smirk away. "Thank you," said Jane for a final time.

Lauren met her eyes and blinked a few times more, like she was processing Jane's reaction. Or non-reaction.

In the past, any action of Lauren's, especially during the decline of their relationship and its immediate aftermath, had set Jane spinning off like a billiard ball that had been whacked firmly by the cue. Lauren must have liked doing it, or why else would she have spent so much time and energy ricocheting into different areas of Jane's life?

Now, Lauren's strike passed right through her with no damage. Like Lauren was smoke, or a ghost, and Jane was flesh, blood, a being in full colour, ready to take on life's next adventure.

Jane turned on her heel and walked off.

Out of the corner of her eye, she thought she saw Lauren make a motion to clasp onto her sleeve, as if to stop her from going. She didn't even consider turning back. She kept on walking.

Back at her desk, she read a new text from Amber. It was about positive energy, manifestations, good vibes sent her way via the astral plane all the way from Sydney.

Jane grinned and sent a text back saying she was looking forward to speaking to her tonight. It wasn't a throwaway line either. If she thought about the next few hours, telling Amber about Lauren's weirdness was an event almost on par with the panel interview she had been working towards her whole adult life.

She grabbed her apple and took a big bite. It was a good one, sweet and juicy. It was a positive omen going into her interview. And she still had enough time to gather her thoughts. Lauren hadn't really been that much of an inconvenience after all.

She turned her chair and looked out at the blue autumn sky, wishing she had a time travel machine to go back to her past self from a year ago, agonising and worrying about Lauren, trying to get to the bottom of why she did the things she did and how love could get so twisted up and painful.

Lauren not even registering as an inconvenience? *Now, that's progress.*

Jane took another bite and started reading through her preparatory notes one last time.

CHAPTER 24

"I really could have ordered an Uber," said Jane as she got into the passenger seat of Teddy's car. Well, Jane supposed it was a hire car as they were in Melbourne and Teddy didn't live there. *Where does he live?* Jane thought about asking him that, but this was chased up by another thought about where Amber lived. LA? Sydney? Jane loved dating Amber, but the thought of her changing anything about her life because of Jane still made Jane's chest tighten.

Amber had insisted on Teddy picking Jane up at the airport. She said it was worth it to see Jane seconds earlier than otherwise. It crossed Jane's mind that it was kind of silly that Teddy—whom she had no issue with but also nothing in common with—could come and pick her up, but Jane's rule that Amber could not collect her from the airport was still in force. She wondered if there was some part of Amber that wanted to make this point, which was why she had sent Teddy.

Jane sighed. *Not everyone has ulterior motives.* It would take a while to unlearn her lessons from being with Lauren for so many years. Besides, it wouldn't be long until Jane learned about the associate professor role. Then there was no reason she couldn't hold hands with Amber out in the world. Public displays of affection—it would be open season.

Her jaw tensed for a moment. Would she really be OK with that? She shook her head. There was no use thinking about any of this until she heard about the job. It would be counting her chickens before they had their birth announcement on the front cover of *Women's Day* magazine.

"How did your big job interview go?" Teddy asked.

"It went well, thank you. I answered every question in full, and there were no surprises. I think I managed to demonstrate that I fulfilled all the criteria."

"Slay," he replied.

Jane glanced over at him. She had heard Sara say that, or something similar. Should she ask him what it meant?

He kept his eyes on the road.

She wondered what he thought of her and Amber together. Did he think they were ridiculous, like chalk and cheese? That she was fooling herself that she would be able to keep Amber's attention? "Plain Jane", a mean kid named Celia had called her in primary school.

I bet Celia's not on the brink of becoming associate professor at one of the nation's best universities.

She looked out the window at the big Essendon Fields sign that marked the border into proper Melbourne and wished Celia well, wherever she was. Coming up with original taunts had not been her strong suit, but Jane hoped she had found her calling in life.

They arrived at the hotel, and Teddy drove them down to the undercover car park. As the lift shot up, so did Jane's spirits. Amber was here, and they had the whole weekend to spend together. Well, except for when Amber had to be the prematch entertainment at the A-League women's soccer grand final, but apart from that, she would have her all to herself.

When the lift opened, Teddy handed Jane her suitcase and said his room was down the hall. He pointed Jane in the direction of Amber's room with a smile and gave a small wave before he walked off.

Jane knocked and her heart started pounding as she heard running footsteps and someone fumbling with the door from the inside.

"Jane!" Amber beamed and launched herself.

Jane grabbed her around the middle so hard that she lifted her up off the ground.

Amber kissed her, and Jane spun her around before walking her into the hotel room.

With her feet back on the ground Amber brushed her hair back from her face and laughed. "Jeez, that was straight out of a rom-com. We need to greet each other like that every time."

Jane bent to give her one more kiss on the mouth. "Oh, absolutely. When I get back from fetching a dozen eggs from IGA."

"Or a litre of milk and a *Women's Day* from the servo."

The unexpected picture of absolute domesticity struck Jane. She wanted it. But was a life like that with Amber even possible?

"I missed you," said Jane.

"Awww, I missed you too. So much. I especially missed these cans!" She ran her hand with purpose from Jane's waist to her breast and had a cheeky grope.

Jane's body thrilled at Amber's touch.

Amber pressed her body against Jane's and looked up at her. "We've got an hour until the car gets here to take us to the game." Her breath played across Jane's jaw. "Is that enough time?"

Jane took her in her arms and kissed her neck. "I'm very keen. *Really* very keen. An hour will be more than enough. We could even have a cup of tea after."

Amber untucked Jane's shirt roughly. "Bloody excellent."

Jane had indigestion from a stadium meat pie. She should have gone for the Greek salad, but she didn't know if she could trust the feta cheese that had been sitting behind glass for heavens knew how long.

The grand final match of the season was a local derby between Melbourne City and Melbourne Victory. It was a sellout, with more than 40,000 people there on a fine but cool afternoon.

Jane was by no means a sports nut, but she knew that women's soccer had become wildly popular in Australia. A lot of people at work had started talking to her about the national team, the Matildas, assuming that because Jane was a lesbian she knew a lot about team sports. They were quickly put right by Jane's complete ignorance of any of it. She was enjoying the atmosphere at this match, though. She was sure Amber would say the vibes were good. She would have to ask her when she got there.

Amber's prematch performance had started out strong. Jane even sung along to some of the words. The melodies were still a foreign language to her, but she was now able to tell most of the songs apart.

The stadium had "gone off"—another term she had picked up from Sara. It stuck in her brain because *gone off* was something bad that happened to tubs of yoghurt she forgot about in the fridge; interesting that it could also be a positive thing.

Jane watched Amber strut and dance across the stage, of course, but she also looked around at the crowd a lot during the performance. When she had attended Amber's performances before, they had been in darkened theatres, but today, in the brilliant afternoon sunshine, it was intoxicating to watch people sing and dance along, having the time of their lives. A family a couple of rows back had two mums about Jane's age, with kids about ten or twelve years old. All of them knew every lyric. The kids must have been raised on Amber's music.

Jane shook her head in wonderment. Amber really meant a lot to so many people. It was impossible to argue that what she created didn't matter. Unless happiness and fun didn't matter.

Who are these imaginary people, making the argument that popular entertainment doesn't matter? Jane winced when she realised her theoretical debate opponent was her old self from before her trip to LA. Was she really such a killjoy? Her body of knowledge was anthropology and sociology, but she posed herself a psychological question: Could people really change? Had she changed?

She felt happier in the last few months since she had met Amber. Maybe the happiest she had ever felt since childhood. Sure, the heady days of being a uni student and falling in love with her line of study were happy times. And things had been good with Lauren, until they hadn't.

Jane had always found joy in pursuing knowledge and truth, but there was another kind of important joy that she was just beginning to learn about: fun.

The crowd roared as Amber launched into another song. The people in front and to either side of her jumped to their feet. She stood too, so she could watch Amber's performance instead of instead of strangers' grooving bottoms.

Jane recognised the song's beat. There was a repeated part with loud drums then a "whoa-oh". She smiled as she anticipated one of the "whoa-ohs" and was able to sing along.

The people in front jumped and held both arms up as they also joined in.

Jane was much more restrained.

Amber was working everyone up into a frenzy, holding up her microphone and yelling, "Come on, come on!"

Jane tapped her foot. Everyone else in the stand seemed like they were moving as one, united by pure enjoyment. People swayed and jumped, flinging their arms and yelling the lyrics. She couldn't tell, but she was sure not every one of them could have been in tune. But they didn't care how they sounded.

For the first time, Jane wished she could let go and dance. She patted her hand against her leg in time with her foot that still tapped. The song reached a crescendo, and she wanted to wiggle her shoulders and sway her hips like the people around her were doing, but something stopped her. She willed herself to move.

The song ended.

The crowd clapped and whooped.

Amber bowed and blew kisses to them, her arms flung wide like she wanted to embrace all of the thousands and thousands of the people there.

Jane clapped until her hands hurt. Applause—that she could do.

She sat back down in her uncomfortable plastic seat. *Ok, so people can change. But not all at once.*

The first half was well underway before Amber and Teddy appeared at the end of Jane's row, followed closely by a broad-shouldered woman in a black suit. Their seats were in a sectioned-off area, where servers brought trays of drinks and canapés and the plastic seats had little fold-down tables like the lecture hall at the university.

There was a smattering of applause as people noticed Amber.

"We're so glad you've come home!" someone called out. It was the family Jane had seen earlier.

Home? Jane thought the cavernous concrete stadium in Melbourne, a city where Amber had never lived, was a funny place to describe as "home." They must have been talking about Australia in general.

Amber thanked everyone in turn as they shifted their knees to let her pass by. "Hi," she said as she sat down, puffing out her cheeks and exhaling. She smiled at Jane but did not make a move to kiss her.

Jane's tummy twinged. Her boundaries were being adhered to. But was she starting to hate them? If so, then who was the authority upholding them with such discipline?

"Are you OK, Miss Hatfield?" the woman in black asked.

"Yes. Thank you, Lavender. All good."

Lavender bumped hard against some spectators' knees as she moved back down the row. She stood on the stairs and scanned her eyes back and forth over the people in Amber's general vicinity.

"Hi," Jane said to Amber. She nodded at Teddy, who sat down on her other side, then smiled back at Amber. "Your show was really good. Everyone was dancing." She flicked her eyes towards the security guard. "I see you've gained a new friend."

"Oh yes, Lavender." Amber raised her eyes heavenwards for just a moment. "A bit of overkill, if you ask me, but Teddy insisted."

"Uh, yah," he said. "I did some judo as a kid, but don't count on me if there's a stampede of crazed fans anytime soon." He took a big bite of meat pie.

Amber rubbed Jane's upper arm. "You're sweet about the show. Yeah, the energy was amped. I had an amazing time with this one, actually. Small venues over in the States are great. In some of the smaller cities, I do really intimate shows where it feels like I see every single person's face and connect with them. But a massive stadium as a venue? I enjoyed it more than I thought I would. I felt like Taylor Swift up there!"

Jane cleared her throat. "What you mean to say is, you're in your Stadium Era?" She folded her hands in her lap.

Teddy choked on soft drink and pounded his chest with his fist.

Amber's eyebrows shot up as she spluttered with laughter. "Hold on. Did you just serve a semi-recent popular culture reference-slash-joke?"

"You've come a long way, baby," said Teddy, still coughing.

Jane's insides glowed.

The crowd made a collective noise as a player wearing sky blue, with her hair in a bun on top of her head, streaked down the sideline with the ball.

Jane felt at one with the big crowd that had gathered there today to watch Amber's show and this big game of soccer. She had never taken part in the things that everyone else got excited about, focusing her time and energy on her work instead.

A short-haired woman from the other team ran to meet the player with the ball. They had a stand-off near the corner of the pitch, then the attacker tried to get around the defender with some very fancy footwork. The defender got a toe to the ball, but the attacker was able to get a pass away towards the goal. A striker for the sky-blue team got a boot to it, but the shot was blocked by the goalie.

The scoreboard display stayed with the pair in the corner as they jogged back towards the middle. They were talking, the attacker smiling, the defender rolling her eyes.

"They're a couple, those two," Teddy told Jane.

"Wow, hitting us with the unexpected sports knowledge there," said Amber.

Teddy rolled his eyes, just like the short-haired woman on the screen. "I know about sports when they're interesting and have drama. Women's soccer is better than *Real Housewives* a lot of the time, especially when you have friends that can give you the behind-the-scenes goss."

"Constantly competing against each other with everyone watching, must be a challenge for them," said Jane. "I wonder if it's hard."

Amber looked up at the screen. "It seems to me like it's worth it," she said.

Amber was right. Even if easier options existed for these women, their faces, huge and pixelated on the scoreboard, looked like they wouldn't want to be anywhere else in the world.

The image changed, and Jane blinked rapidly as her own face appeared. Panic surged. The crowd got noisy again, and people near her laughed. Everyone's eyes were on her. She ducked down and grabbed Teddy's arm, dragging him sideways to sit next to Amber, as she took his seat instead, out of the camera's frame. She leant sideways, pressing against the man next to her so that even her shoulder wasn't being broadcast.

"Amber, Amber, Amber," some sections of the crowd chanted.

Amber waved at the screen, then spotted the camera like a true pro and pointed and smiled right down the barrel. She made a love heart shape with her hands, and people cheered.

The screen flicked back to the game as the goalie kicked the ball back in.

Amber's smile was gone as she turned towards Jane.

Now that the glare of the metaphorical spotlight wasn't on her, Jane's chest fell and went cold. She had been rude, squirming away. She hoped she hadn't hurt Amber's feelings. "Sorry, I..." She trailed off because she couldn't think of any explanation that wouldn't make it worse.

She didn't like being looked at without her permission at the best of times. Up in front of a full lecture theatre was different—that was her arena, her stadium. She sighed. Maybe Lauren had gotten in her head after all, about the job and the panel. There was a part of her that felt on edge about jetting off to a sports match with her superstar girlfriend instead of hunching over her computer all weekend, marking papers and humbly waiting for a decision from the powers on high.

Amber nodded. "It's OK," she said and turned back to watch the game.

Teddy looked straight ahead too, completely still, like a lump of rock between her and Amber.

She slumped back in her seat, tears pricking her eyes. She had ruined it. The fun, the energy, the happiness, all spoiled because she didn't want people to see her and have opinions.

She balled her fist and made a resolution. *After I get this job, I'm not going to care what anyone else thinks of me. I'm going to do what I want.*

The teary feeling went away. *I can be like those soccer women. I can have the job, the relationship, all of it.*

Teddy shifted in his seat beside her, looking for all the world like a Victorian chaperone plonked down between two young lovers. Except these lovers sat in unhappy silence.

Only a few more days.

CHAPTER 25

Melbourne Victory won the match. Amber received a text from one of the players, Keeley, the short-haired woman in the couple Teddy had told Jane about. She invited Amber to the locker room to celebrate with the team. What Teddy hadn't revealed to Jane was that Keeley and Amber had been friends for a few years, following a very brief fling. It wasn't a massive secret, and she had had every intention of telling Jane before Jane had done her Houdini act and jumped away from Amber like she was an oncoming Spencer Street tram. The rest of the match had been awkward, with Teddy sat between them radiating discomfort.

Jane had her reasons. Being the centre of attention made her want to curl up into a little ball. It wasn't natural to her. And this job process was important to her—the culmination of her life's work. Amber understood all of this. But Jane's actions still stung like a rejection. It was like being seen with Amber, having people know they were together, was the worst thing that could happen to her.

Amber entered the wild party, flanked by Teddy and Lavender, with Jane a step behind. She knew she should pull Jane aside and tell her about her history with Keeley, but the yelling and whooping in the locker room was a deafening wall of sound. Plus, her relationship with Keeley had started out as a one-night stand but over the years had become a steady friendship, with no weirdness or tension. Amber had met Keeley's partner, Christine, who was tough as nails and would have made no bones about it if she had any issue with her.

The scene before her was chaos. Players in various states of undress swigged champagne straight from the bottle or paper cups. In a huddle in the middle of the room, players had their arms flung around each other's shoulders and were singing Kylie Minogue's "Better the Devil You Know" at the top of their voices.

Amber chuckled. Nobody on the team had been born when that song came out.

She took Jane's hand and squeezed it. "You OK?"

Jane nodded, squeezing back. She looked a bit like a stunned mullet as she surveyed the wildness of the room, crowded to the edges with player's families and team staff. She was smiling, though.

Amber's spirits rose. A few months ago, Jane would have been wincing at this noise and crush of people. Maybe there was hope of them meeting in the middle after all.

Amber was yanked sideways into a bear hug.

"You're a sight for sore eyes, mate!" said Keeley as she released her. "Sorry about the sweat."

"No worries, Mac," Amber replied with her friend's old nickname. "Good win out there. You played well."

Keeley grinned. "We all did. Hey." She jumped up on a bench and put her hands to her face like a megaphone. "Oi, we've got music royalty in the house, Vics," she yelled. "Amber Hatfield has come to join the party!"

Everyone in the room clapped and yelled.

Keeley pulled her by the hand up onto the bench. Everyone hushed.

"I had to come and congratulate you legends," Amber said. "Amazing work today, all your hard work has paid off. It was an absolute honour to sing for your crowd. A massive crowd that broke the all-time domestic record for a women's football match, and they got to see you win—win the whole fucking thing!"

The room erupted in a roar. Amber and Keeley jumped down and were pulled into photo after photo, with people's mums, nannas, physios—it seemed everyone wanted a piece of them. Lavender stood behind Amber's left shoulder during every interaction.

Keeley beamed for everyone, knew everyone's auntie's names, and cracked jokes. Her excited smile was infectious.

Amber's cheeks hurt, and she wondered why until she realised she was grinning along with her friend.

After a while, Amber scanned the room to find Jane. She was standing against the wall, a still spot amongst all the merriment, dressed in her dark jeans and black jacket. She took a sip from a paper cup and made a face.

Amber smiled. Maybe it was warm champagne mixed with watermelon Gatorade.

Amber's smile dissipated along with some of the excitement she had been swept up in.

The frown Jane had made when she tasted her drink had not entirely gone away. Her eyes darted, then met Amber's. Jane pressed her lips together in a brave smile.

Amber raised her hand in a wave. Behind her and on either side, people revelled, so happy at what had been achieved that day. The camera flashes, smiles, and countless strangers weren't Amber's whole job, but they were a big part of it. Just like these soccer players—they didn't get to celebratory days like these without personal, solitary training and toil. The fans and well-wishers were an important aspect of it, though. It meant their work could bring joy and inspiration to people, and that made everything sweeter.

She walked to Jane and stood next her, her back to the wall.

Lavender took a big step sideways away from them.

Amber thanked her inwardly. Not all her security personnel had known when to keep a respectful distance.

Jane bent her head to Amber's ear so she could be heard. "I'm really sorry about before. The last thing I want to do is make you unhappy."

Amber sighed. The apology was nice. She had been upset, and she could tell Jane was genuine. Her heaviness shifted a little. "It's OK."

"It's not OK. I'm going to do better. Once the job is decided on. It's going to be soon. Then I can be who you need me to be. I can be more like your ex over there." She gestured towards Keeley, who was hoisted up on two teammates' shoulders. Her neck was bent at a weird angle because her head kept hitting the ceiling, and she was red in the face from laughter.

Amber pressed her lips together. "Teddy told you, hey?"

"Yes. It's not that I mind, don't get me wrong. I was watching the two of you, though, and I wondered if someone more like that—I mean—someone who is in their element at something like this, would be easier for you to be with."

Fear stabbed at Amber. She had been broken up with before. Was this the start of Jane ending it? "Jane, wait, I—"

"It's like the soccer couple, though. There are probably people it would be easier for them to be with. But the heart doesn't choose logic, or weigh up the pros and cons. I acknowledge I'm not easy, but once I'm not under professional scrutiny like this, I'm going to try harder. I want to invest in this, in us, if you want to as well?"

Warmth oozed through Amber, melting the cold fear away. She stood toe to toe with Jane and looked into her eyes. "Sign me up. I don't have much liquid cash on hand, but I can invest my full set of astral cosmic crystals, today if you want."

Jane smiled and put her hands on Amber's hips, bending to kiss her on the mouth. The kiss was soft, with just the faintest brush of tongue on her lip.

Amber's toes curled. She ran her hands up Jane's back and held her. The noise of the party disappeared, and all she could hear was her own heartbeat in her ears.

The kiss ended, and Amber looked around like she was drunk. The soundtrack of the wild celebrations was back, but she didn't feel like it was her world anymore.

She and Jane turned to watch the party. Jane put her arm around her shoulders, and Amber scooched in and hugged Jane's waist. The energy from the party pumped all around them. It was like they were in an invisible pod where the air hummed with a quiet calm.

She leant her head against Jane's shoulder. Maybe she would rejoin the noisy press of people in a bit, if they played a song she couldn't resist dancing to. For the moment, the best fun she could think of was staying put right where she was.

CHAPTER 26

Jane refreshed the airline's app once more as she fumbled behind the bedside table to unplug her charger.

Amber lay in bed, arm flung across her eyes.

Jane paused to look at her a moment as she walked to her bag. It was the day after the soccer game, and she had to fly back in time for an afternoon meeting at work. Monday mornings, any morning really, held no meaning for Amber. Her life was so different. Jane's was a steady inexorable pattern of weeks, terms, semesters—breaks differentiated by family meals (ham at Christmas and lamb at Easter) and the weather, but pretty much the same year after year.

What must it be like to move like quicksilver from day to day, moving unpredictably depending on whether Teddy's iCal showed a rep meeting at 11:30am or a festival set at 10:45pm? Or a day spent plucking guitar strings or plinking at piano keys, trying to tap into the well of mysterious creativity within?

Amber's eyes fluttered open. "Why don't ya take a picture, it'll last longer." She grinned sleepily and rolled onto her stomach towards Jane.

"I'm taking a mental picture, for later use when I'm missing you back in Brisbane." She sat on the edge of the bed and bent to kiss Amber's shoulder blade.

"Aw. I woke up sassy, and you're all sugar." She wrapped her arms around Jane's waist and pulled her head up onto Jane's lap. "You gotta jet, hey?"

"Yes, unfortunately. I'll text you when I land and phone you tonight, OK?" She smiled and stroked Amber's hair. Amber's head became heavier against her legs as she started to drift off again.

They had both gone to a nightclub with the Melbourne Victory and stayed the same amount of time, but Amber had danced and danced while Jane sat in the beer garden with one of the older player's husbands and talked about Eastern European history. His parents had fled Bosnia, and he had a keen interest in his roots. Jane had many years ago studied the effects of displacement on populations through the lens of 1990s wars and conflicts, and they had a very interesting discussion and exchanged email addresses.

Amber snuffled awake and held up her head. "Text me before you land, you sausage. That's hours and hours away."

Jane grinned. "All right, live-tweet my Uber ride to the airport, will I?" She picked up her phone and tapped with her thumbs. "Right. 'Passing Coles truck on the Tullamarine Freeway.' Um, 'Driver asks if the aircon temperature is OK.' Ah!" The phone rang, and Jane dropped it into the bedsheets. The incoming area code was a Brisbane landline, the number quite similar to her landline number at work.

The uni. Cortisol jolted through her.

She didn't expect to hear from them about the job until Wednesday at the earliest. Maybe this was follow-up questions.

"Hello?"

"Hello, Jane. It's Professor Laramee. I'm phoning in regard to the recent recruitment process for the associate professor position within the social sciences faculty."

Her hands and feet went numb. "Hello Professor. Yes, how are you?"

He ignored her enquiry and continued without pausing. "We have completed the required process and come to a decision."

Amber was sitting up now, wearing Jane's University of Queensland Debate and Mooting Team 2001 T-shirt, which was comically oversized on her. Her eyes were wide. She made a questioning motion with both hands at Jane.

Jane gave a tense nod.

Amber gasped and clasped her hands in front of her.

"The field of candidates was of a very high quality," the professor continued.

Jane's blood pounded in her ears. An icy feeling was descending through her chest. People didn't prevaricate this long with good news.

"Unfortunately, you were among the unsuccessful candidates. The panel took into account your high-quality research outputs and teaching achievements, but another candidate was considered to have met the agreed criteria more comprehensively."

Jane opened her mouth, but no sounds came out. The iciness had spread outwards to her whole body. Her shoulders slumped.

"I'm sorry, Jane," he concluded, sounding for the first time like he wasn't reading off a memorandum. Professor Laramee had worked with her father and had provided Jane valuable mentoring more than once when she was starting out.

"I understand. Thank you for informing me. Goodbye." The phone fell from her hands back into the tangled bedsheets.

She covered her face with her hands, but tears didn't come. Everything was wrong. If she closed her eyes for a minute, maybe she would open them up again and the phone call would have been a stress nightmare—the kind that happen three minutes before an alarm clock goes off at the start of a big day.

Jane wanted to erase the last few minutes, the room she was in, Amber. Her skin was clammy and warm, and she felt like she wanted to jump out of it.

She strode to the window, opened the curtain, and looked out, trying to get some distance between herself and what had just happened.

The hotel room was high up, so Jane was standing above any other windows she could see. Below, the muddy, narrow river wound past an ugly casino and an outdated art gallery.

Jane's breath shuddered as she inhaled. *Years of work and effort, going the extra mile to become associate professor. I may as well not have bothered.*

"Jane, I'm sorry." Amber's voice was small and gentle.

Jane closed her eyes. The disappointment roiling around in her head latched onto Amber's words and formed a reply. *You should be.*

Jane had been on track for years, only good reports of her efforts, only positive relationships with everyone at the uni. Except for the last few months. She had put work second for the first time in her life. And everything had come undone.

"I could have done things differently," she said, her back still to Amber. Her voice was calm and cold despite the turmoil inside her.

"You don't know that," Amber said.

Jane wheeled around. "I do know. You're correct that the outcome still could have remained the same; we don't have all the information. But the fact remains that I could have limited my distractions, been more conscientious."

Amber went over to Jane and put one hand to her cheek. "Hey, we can never know everything that's going on. There are factors outside our control. You never know, maybe there was never any way you were getting the job. You can't blame yourself."

Jane took Amber's wrist and removed her hand from her face. She took a couple of backwards steps to the door. "I was getting it. I was so sure. Everything was lined up. But you pushed me, you made this more serious than it was meant to be. I put you first, even though we'd just met. I was crazy agreeing to a full-blown long-distance relationship. I should have put you off." Jane ran her fingers through her hair and paced back and forth. Sadness and powerlessness were being replaced with something hot and fierce, and Jane ran with it. It was relief.

"I could have said 'I'll call you mid-year—only a few months, look, only really a matter of weeks'. But you wanted something from me right away. Also, you followed me and set yourself up in Australia even though I didn't ask you to. I didn't ask for any of this!"

She stopped pacing and faced Amber.

Amber looked smaller than usual in her oversized T-shirt. She didn't make a move to approach Jane again. She stood stock-still next to the window. Her eyes blazed. "I think you had better go," she said, her voice thick but not wavering.

Go. Jane's eyes scanned the room. Her bags were already packed. She'd double-checked the bathroom drawers for forgotten toiletries. It was time to leave for the airport anyway.

Her eyes fell on Amber again.

Amber's cheeks were flushed, and she held her shoulders tense.

Go...and leave Amber here unhappy?

The thundering rush of blood in Jane's head slowed a notch, but it only meant the sear of disappointment flared up stronger than before.

She's always needing something. Something I'm not able to give, to be. "I can't pretend I'm fine," Jane said, not moving from her spot by the door.

Amber lifted her chin and closed her eyes. She seemed to shrink even further. "Nobody's asking you to," she said. "I'm just asking you to go." She opened her eyes, and they were shiny from tears.

Jane's eyes stung too. She started to raise her hand to reach out and do something about Amber's sadness. *She said go. She doesn't want you.*

Jane grabbed her suitcase and shoulder bag and reached for the door. She stopped for a second and closed her eyes. *Maybe I'll never see Amber again. Ever again.*

The mad whirl of emotions reached a fever pitch. Fear and sadness and anger. Her unhappiness and Amber's unhappiness.

It was all too much.

Facts. That was her safe space. Amber had told her to go, so she would go.

She pushed the door open and walked out without looking back.

CHAPTER 27

Teddy crashed through the door as Amber unlocked it. "Babes!" He wrapped her in a hug, and she burst into tears. "Awwwwww." He rubbed her back.

"Why does this keep happening to me?" Amber asked, her voice muffled by sobs and also the candy-striped shirt Teddy was wearing, that she had pressed her face into. She felt like she had been sideswiped by a city bus out of nowhere. Two hours ago, she and Jane had been in bed together, kissing and pillow talking. What had happened? Amber could never have imagined the angry figure Jane had become, throwing barbs to hurt her.

"Your text just said you and Jane had a fight and she left. But I *know* she's fucking dead to me and you're a total angel." He gave her a squeeze. "I'll make you a cup of tea."

She eventually calmed down enough to give him a rundown of Jane's phone call from the uni and everything that followed.

Teddy leaned his head to one side and made his fingers a contemplative pyramid in front of his face. He took a deep breath. "She's fucking dead to me. Call my personal morgue and funeral director. Stone-cold."

Amber closed her eyes, and silent tears started to fall again. "I don't know. Maybe I reacted badly? She got really terrible news about the job. Did I make it about me?"

Teddy took her by the shoulders. "Listen. Jane straight-up blamed you for her missing out on becoming Professor Plum or whatever. That's messed up. Making you out to be some lovesick puppy that followed her around everywhere. I've seen the two of you. It was her that looked like that love-heart-eyes emoji half the time.

"This the first time you've seen her in a tight spot, and guess what, she acted worse than a drunk villain at a *Real Housewives* reunion. When people tell you who they really are, babe, you gotta believe them."

Amber slumped sideways and hid her face in the bedsheets. Teddy was right. She had spent most of her adolescence justifying her mother's behaviour to herself. Because if the most important person in her life was nothing but a self-obsessed, greedy narcissist, that meant she didn't have anybody.

She should have cut her mother off many years before she did. The lesson had been hard-won, but she had learned it well.

Now she was hollowed out.

She had pictured the next few weeks and months filled with Jane, phone calls, visits, and making plans for the future. A dull exhaustion settled over her when she thought about what it might look like now. "So what, then? Is the whole thing over?" Her face scrumpled with sadness.

Teddy rubbed her back in soothing circles. "I can't tell you that, honey. What would she need to do? Come crawling back to you on her knees saying it will never happen again? Would you believe her?"

Amber didn't reply. The look on Jane's face before she'd walked out the door was burned into her memory. She couldn't imagine that face soft and pleading for forgiveness. She had let Jane get too close to the most vulnerable part of her, and now it seemed like she didn't know her at all.

She flinched and sat upright as the phone on the bedside table started to ring.

Teddy grabbed it, and his eyebrows shot up as she read the name on the screen. He held it out to Amber wordlessly.

Jane.

Amber pressed her fingertips against the bridge of her nose. She wasn't ready to be hurt again. But this brink of yawning emptiness was no fun either. She took the phone and pressed the green button, but she couldn't speak. She didn't know which version of Jane was on the other end.

"Amber?" The voice was loud and strained. There was a lot of background noise.

"Yes." The word came out small and flat, even though hope and fear were at war inside her chest.

"They're about to call my flight to board."

Amber closed her eyes and breathed. She wasn't going to send this conversation skittering in one direction or another. It was up to Jane.

"I don't like how we left things," said Jane.

A flicker of Amber's anger returned. *Sure, things were left really shitty. By you.*

"I'm—" Jane began, then was drowned out by an intercom announcement about a flight.

"What was that? I couldn't hear you?"

"Amber, hello?"

"Yes, I'm here. You were saying? Did you say you were sorry?"

"Sorry? No. I didn't say I was sorry." There was a brief reprieve from the babble of announcements, with just relative silence on the other end of the line.

Amber stayed silent too. Her chest and throat felt white-hot.

"Are you there?" asked Jane.

"You don't like how we left things, but you're not sorry? Did you want me to be sorry? I know you got some bad news, but that's no excuse to lash out at me. Or do I have it wrong? Do you really think I manipulated you against your will into dating me, and you were just laying out true facts? Do I mean anything to you at all? Because right now, you seem pretty comfortable with calling the whole thing off."

Jane didn't reply.

Through the phone there was random airport babble and the shrieking of an unknown child.

"I..." Jane began.

A cold dullness settled in Amber's stomach.

Jane cleared her throat, the sound harsh through the phone. "Can we talk later? In private? There are just, so many, um, a lot of people here."

Amber dropped her head and closed her eyes. *And there it is.* Jane would rather have Amber sit in abject misery, the colour leeching out of her soul, for hours, than have a few random strangers raise an eyebrow at her for showing human emotion.

"You know, later isn't going to work for me," said Amber, steel in her voice. "The thing is, if you're in my life, there's always going to be people around. There's always going to be eyes directed our way. Don't get me wrong: I'm not asking that you love it. In some ways, actually, it was really nice that you weren't addicted to the attention.

"I understand it's a challenge for you. I get that being with me is challenge after challenge. And I learned today that you don't handle challenges well. You're pretty shit at it.

"I just wanted..." She trailed off and drew in a shuddering breath as the tears came. "When a challenge came, when it suddenly wasn't easy anymore, I thought you would step up." Her voice was betraying her, getting higher and thinner. "You never did, Jane. Maybe it's best I learned this now, rather than months or years down the track. What did we have, really? Just a handful of overnight dates. If you're going to leave, just go."

"Amber, please," said Jane quietly.

Amber waited, giving Jane every chance.

The seconds slid by.

Through the phone there was just anonymous airport hubbub.

"Goodbye, Jane." She ended the call. Teddy rushed to sit bedside her, catching her in his arms just in time.

She sobbed into his neck, not tears of anger, just bitter disappointment.

CHAPTER 28

The lights went out in Jane's office at the university, and she jumped up and waved her arms in the air.

After 9pm, the lights in the smaller offices were operated by motion sensor, and it was nearly an hour past nine.

The lights came back on with a clicking noise. Jane did a couple of star jumps for good measure. Her eyes felt like they were full of sand.

She looked out her window at the darkened campus. On the ground below, a brushtail possum ran across the footpath and stuck its head in a bin, fishing something out and holding it to its mouth with its little hands. Jane hoped it was an apple core and not the remains of a hot dog or Mars bar.

She folded her arms and rocked back on her heels, thinking that she really ought to go home, but she didn't want to face her empty place, her suitcase still open, unpacked from her return from Melbourne a couple of days earlier.

It didn't make any sense—Amber hadn't spent much time in Jane's townhouse, but the absence of her, the absence of the *idea* of her and of the possibility that she might call or text at any moment, was deafening.

Jane closed her eyes and massaged her temples. Her feet felt heavy against the floor, like she was full of cold, grey cement.

She replayed the events of a few days before, like she'd been doing nonstop, tiring her brain out, reliving everything like a car crash.

The call from uni, blaming Amber, Amber telling her to go, Amber telling her not to call again.

Jane groaned. She had said unkind things to Amber, things she didn't mean. She didn't believe Amber had forced her into the relationship. She winced. She didn't even remember clearly everything she had said, just flashes of intense feeling—hurt, defensiveness, and an angry, red urge to wreck everything.

Amber had been hurt. The memory of her tears through the phone when Jane had been at the airport still made her want to collapse into a ball of remorse.

Later isn't going to work for me.

The words rang in her head. Amber never wanted to hear Jane's voice again.

The saddest thing was there was a little part of Jane that celebrated and revelled. This tiny, hard part of herself that had known all along that she would ruin it, that she and Amber weren't right for one another. It had known for sure that Jane wasn't good enough for her.

"This is more like the Jane Miles I know."

Jane whirled around.

Lauren leaned against her doorframe, smiling. "Burning the midnight oil. I haven't seen you here at this hour for a while."

"No," Jane replied. She sat down at her desk, a little discombobulated by having to interact when she thought she had been alone.

Lauren, still smiling, detached from the doorframe and approached the desk. She dropped the smile, and her face became a mask of empathetic concern. "I was so sorry to hear about the associate professorship," she said.

Jane blinked. "I didn't think anyone had been told yet. They're still arranging the paperwork."

"You know me. I have my fingers in all the pies." A brief smile played across her face before being replaced with the concerned mask.

Jane slumped in her chair, exhausted to her core. *Is this what my future holds in store? Constant reminders of this failure? And my failure with Amber?* She jumped up and faced the window again, panicked suddenly that she might burst into tears in front of her ex.

She breathed in slowly. The fear of crying passed, replaced again by emptiness, like the edge of outer space.

"It breaks my heart to see you like this." Lauren had sidled up beside her, and her voice, closer than Jane expected, made her jump. "I know our break-up was very hard for you, but you seemed to be doing better, moving on. You even started something new with…your pickleball."

The pause felt meaningful. Jane's stomach had lurched, wondering if Lauren knew more than she was meant to. *No, she's getting in my head again.* She closed her eyes. She *had* been doing better, until she fucked it all up.

Lauren leant against the windowsill, standing right in front of Jane.

Lauren wasn't touching her, but her closeness caused Jane to inhale sharply. Her instinct was to take a step back, but she didn't. She stayed still.

"You don't hate me, do you Jane?" Lauren asked, her voice just louder than a whisper.

"No," said Jane, and it was the truth. She didn't know what she felt, but it was a relief not to be empty for a moment.

Lauren's scent, the shape of her body, was so familiar.

Jane's breath caught again as Lauren ran the fingers of both hands down her belly, resting them lightly on the belt of Jane's pants.

A faint pulse of desire beat through Jane. The skin under her shirt rose into goosebumps, as if her skin recognised Lauren's touch of its own accord.

Lauren stared into her eyes, intent on every expression, every physical reaction. Her touch was like a warm spark in the middle of yawning loneliness.

I could move back into our old house and have our dog again. The image of the house they had shared ran through her mind.

She took a step back. *The house. The fights, the silence, the emotional warfare.* The old wounds started to ache, driving out any tenderness.

She took Lauren's wrists, removing the hands from her waist. "I don't hate you, but I think you had better go."

Lauren's mouth dropped open. "Wh-wh-wha..." she spluttered, then trailed off, balling her hands into fists. Her eyes darted, then flashed.

She stalked past Jane, knocking her shoulder on the way past.

At the doorway, Lauren turned back. Her face was pale except for two red spots on her cheeks. "I hope it's all worth the cost, Jane. I really do." She swung around and was gone.

Jane sat down on the desk with a *thump.* She ran her hand through her hair, breathing a deep sigh. She was scared at how close she had come to toppling off a massive cliff onto the jagged rocks below. She had grabbed a tree branch at the last minute. It could have been a lot worse.

Lauren's parting words echoed in her head. *Worth the cost.* Did she mean the cost of spurning her advances tonight? It didn't really make any sense.

Moving on. Something unpleasant turned in Jane's stomach. *Fingers in all the pies.*

What did Lauren know?

Jane followed the line of logic of a new theory taking root in her mind. If Lauren had found out about Jane moving on, it would have driven her crazy. In some periods of their relationship, she had been distant and withholding, but in other phases she had been possessive and jealous.

Worth the cost.

What if Lauren had been the one to make her pay?

CHAPTER 29

"Please take a seat. Would you like Clarissa to bring you a glass of water?"

"No, thank you," Jane replied. She addressed Clarissa, Professor Whittaker's administrative assistant, as Clarissa left the room and received a smile and nod of acknowledgement in return. "I appreciate you meeting with me, Professor."

"Not at all. We encourage unsuccessful applicants to seek feedback about the process. It can be a valuable learning experience for those seeking to progress and gain greater seniority. As panel chair, I will provide this feedback on behalf of all selection panel members."

Jane had a twinge of impatience and shifted in her chair. The professor never used three words when he could use dozens. His office was lined with shelves of leather-bound books, and his desk was dark and heavy. Jane wondered how he avoided having his spirit oppressed, spending so much time in there. Even the top of his balding head was covered with patches of fine, dark down, like old dust.

"I understand. What is the panel's feedback, please?"

He steepled his fingers in front of his mouth and cleared his throat. "Straight into it, I see. A very direct woman indeed. Well, your research and teaching experience is of a very high standard, equal at least to the other candidates, even though you are younger. Your dedication and long years of service to this institution was noted positively by the panel."

He paused.

Jane nodded, annoyed by the delay. *Does he want a thankyou card? It's all true so far. So why didn't I get the job?*

He cleared his throat again and took a sip from a glass of water. "Yes, yes. Now, this being said, the panel felt some of the other candidates demonstrated the ability to, uh, protect and, well, enhance the culture of the university." He became very interested in lining up a fountain pen perpendicular to the edge of his desk. "Culture is very important."

Jane glared, waiting for him to meet her eyes.

He finally did and then flinched a little.

"Tell me, specifically, what element of my application demonstrated to the panel that I would not 'protect and enhance' the culture?" she asked, each word dropping like a ball bearing.

The professor splayed his fingers on the table and dropped his eyes. "Huh! Well, it's not that there's anything that can be specifically pointed to, per se, in your application. It's more, you see, a matter of demonstrated potential, possible, degradation of the perception of the educational institution."

"Degradation?" Jane repeated. Puzzle pieces were falling into place in her mind, and she didn't like the picture.

"Oh, no, no, no! I misspoke. Not a degradation as such. More of a—how to put this—an obfuscation. Yes, yes—reputational obfuscation."

Jane had had enough. She planted her feet and gripped her knees. "You talk about the culture of this place. I *am* the culture. I have lived and breathed this place my entire life. My students love me. My research is well-regarded internationally."

"Naturally, naturally. That's difficult to deny. However—"

Jane held up a hand, and he snapped his mouth shut.

"Tell me, plainly, if the fact I'm a lesbian is the thing that is so degrading to everyone," she said.

He clasped his hands, as if pleading with her. "No! Not at all. The university values and celebrates all sexualities and genders. We don't mind that you're gay. I was happy to come to your housewarming party when Lauren invited me. Remember? I brought the 2007 chablis!"

Jane sat forward. "Then what? What is the issue?"

He wiped beads of sweat from his head and rifled through some papers on his desk. "There's nothing specific in your application I can point to," he said, then took a deep breath. "The other applicants included more demonstrable potential for the culture piece during the process. And it would be very improper—in fact, illegal under the Privacy Act—for me to divulge to you the details of someone else's job application. I'm afraid, Jane, that's all there is to it."

Jane had an involuntary urge to concede. It had happened too many times before. It was the tried and tested process—her expression of something she wanted, pushback from her superiors, and acceptance of the situation.

But this time there was a short-circuit.

The automatic cycle didn't kick in.

No.

"Not good enough, Ronald," she said with deadly calm.

"I beg your pardon?"

A quiet power surged within her, so strong that she rose to her feet. "Either I leave here today knowing the truth or we do this the hard way. You're yanking my chain—you know it and I know it. Tell me why I didn't get the job or I'll slap you with a Right to Information request so hard you won't be able to see straight. I'll RTI your emails, texts, everything. Same goes for everyone else on your panel. I'll RTI your goddamn diaries and dream journals if I have to.

"Spill, Ronald, or I'll rain a holy hell down on you and this whole place."

His eyes darted from side-to-side, and Jane knew she had him. There *was* something to hide.

"OK, OK. I'll tell you," he whispered, fingers scrabbling on the surface of his big desk. "You have to know I'll deny this conversation if anyone asks. But I'll tell you, all right?" He closed his eyes and hung his head for a moment before continuing. "Certain material from the internet was brought to my attention some days ago. Photographs that had been posted, of you and a popular music artist embracing and, uh, kissing, in a hallway somewhere. People—members of the public—had commented. The forum was called, um, Seenit? Reddit! Yes, that was it.

"These public commenters were trying to get to the bottom of who you were. It was brought to my attention that it would not take much for a student or someone else to recognise you, and then the university's name would be dragged into the realm of trashy tabloid journalism.

"There's no going back once the cat is out of the bag with something like that. If Australia had an Ivy League, we're not in it, but we're so close."

He held up his fingers to demonstrate just how close he thought it was. "To get those big-fish, super-rich overseas students, we need to demonstrate gravitas and dignity. Those type of parents want their kids' degrees to be taken seriously. You do understand, don't you?"

She sat back down with a bump, and her shoulders sagged. "Was it just you that saw this or the whole panel?" she asked, her voice hollow and without its previous fire.

"The panel were shown. By me. This place is important to you, I know that. I was trying to protect it, to protect us."

The foundations she had built her whole life on were crumbling around her. It wasn't just this one old nutter who clung on to meaningless ideas and didn't know how sub-Reddits worked—the whole panel of her peers and colleagues had bought into it. *This* was the culture. Snobbery, elitism, and greed.

The photos were probably from backstage at the APRA awards, but it was irrelevant at the end of the day. Any public display of affection she and Amber had partaken in, that anyone was able to snap an opportunistic photo of, would have been completely chaste and G-rated.

It was all so stupid. All the effort she had wasted on keeping Amber a secret, and it was all for nothing. The missed opportunities to show the world she was proud to be Amber's person seemed like tragedies now.

I only have myself to blame for how I behaved.

She had one more question, but she already knew the answer. "Who showed you the website?"

Professor Whittaker's chin sunk into his chest, and his eyes darted again, as if weighing up if one known threat was deadlier than another. He hesitated. Then his shoulders sagged. "Lauren."

Jane sat back in the chair and stretched out her legs, crossing them at the ankle. She took a long, slow look around the room, as if seeing it for the first time. The professor, when her eyes swept over him, looked small and confused.

She saw the university as a house of cards. One errant breath from someone careless could blow it all down, leaving a flat, scattered mess.

She stood and cleared her throat. "I'm done, Ronald. This place is a stinking, rotten pile of garbage. I thought the point of it all was to teach the students we have as well as we possibly could. And add to the sum of human knowledge through research and the pursuit of greater understanding.

"You lot are just a nest of insecure vipers, crawling over each other to hide your own inadequacies. I could try to fight it, but I'd end up getting sucked down, down into the quagmire. No, thanks." She tugged on her jacket lapels to straighten herself up. "Fuck you, Ronald, and fuck this place. I'm off to do some good with my life."

She let herself out, gave Clarissa a polite nod, and went to pack everything from her office into her car.

CHAPTER 30

Two weeks later, Jane sat at a long table under a poinciana tree, surrounded by a low hum of relaxed chat. It was her mum Kay's seventieth birthday party, held in the backyard of Jane's childhood home in Logan, Queensland. The late-autumn afternoon was warm and sunny, with a perfect cornflower blue sky. The house sat on two acres of land, sloping down to the Logan River. It had been a wet autumn so far, so everything was beautiful and green.

Jane shifted a piece of roasted heirloom carrot from one side of her plate to the other with her fork. She took another sip of wine. Her brain told her it was delicious, a pinot noir from the Yarra Valley, hers and her mother's favourite drop. But there was no fizz of enjoyment. Nothing.

Her disappointment about how things had ended with Amber had not faded. If anything, her feelings had deepened into a disgust at herself and her actions. In hindsight, it was like someone sinister had been pulling her strings, making her choose wrong move after wrong move. And for what? To protect her chances to move up the ranks in a system that was rotten to the core.

She tried to shift her glum expression into something more party appropriate, but the frown seemed permanent, as if she were a statue carved by a very morose artist.

At the head of the table, her mother let out a scream. "Here's Barbara!"

A small car pulled to a stop on the long gravel driveway, and Barbara, Bill, and Sara got out.

"My precious grandbaby!" yelled Kay and rushed across the lawn. At seventy, she was still very fast and played field hockey weekly.

Jane sighed. As far as Sara, Barbara, and Bill were concerned (Sara was terrible at secrets, so Jane had let her tell her parents about Amber), everything was great with Jane's love life. She would have to break the news.

Or non-news. Jane had not spoken to Amber since she left Melbourne. There had just been a massive silence. Jane was dreading Sara's disappointment. She wasn't sure what her own reaction was going to be. Since nobody else had known about her relationship, it not being there anymore wouldn't make any difference to them.

Her insides were so heavy, she expected her chair legs to sink into the lawn.

A string of party guests trailed after Kay towards the new arrivals.

Jane followed, at the end of the line.

She hugged Barbara last.

As her sister's arms enveloped her, a tiny whimper escaped her mouth.

Barbara stiffened. Without a word, she grabbed Jane's wrist and led her at double pace to a spot near the river behind a stand of bamboo, out of sight and earshot of the rest of the party. "What's wrong?" she asked.

It was the last straw for Jane.

Her jaw went slack.

Her eyes closed. "It's over with Amber."

She held her hand to her nose to stop a sniffle, but she couldn't hold back the body-wracking sob that rose and burst out of her.

Tears spilled.

Barbara pulled her into a wordless hug and rubbed her back, uttering a string of strange noises that, once the outpouring of pent-up misery had held sway for a little while, were surprisingly comforting. "Ohhhhh, ch-ch-ch, dare-d-dare-doh."

Eventually, Jane's shoulders stopped shaking, and she could catch her breath.

"There you are! I've been simply dying. I *need* to hear the latest about—" Sara stopped short when she saw her aunt in tears. "What's wrong?"

"Nobody's injured or unwell, darling. Maybe give us a minute, though," Barbara said.

"No, no. It's OK." Jane said. She had been dreading telling these two about the break-up. *Better to rip the Band-Aid off.* "I was broken up with, that's all. Or, I don't know, maybe I did the breaking? Anyway, the whole thing's been called off."

Sara rubbed her arm and handed her a Pokémon handkerchief.

Jane wiped her eyes, then her entire face (it was all wet), and blew her nose. "Thank you," she said, holding out the hanky.

"You keep that for now," said Sara.

"It was so great, and I ruined it." Her breath caught again, but she fought to retain control.

"Don't worry. They come up fine in the wash. Charmander isn't even my favourite."

"No, with Amber."

Sara winced. "Duh, of course. What happened?"

Jane ran her hand down her face. "I was obsessed with putting a lid on it, making sure strangers on the street wouldn't know we were together. Then I didn't get the associate professorship I applied for, and I blamed her. I said some terrible things. I'd be ashamed to tell you. Then it turns out Lauren *had* told the uni about Amber, and that *was* actually the reason I didn't get the job."

"Hold the freaking phone! What the what?" Sara said.

"You're fucking kidding me!" Barbara said.

Jane sighed. "I know. Look, she was either listening at the door when Sara and I were talking, or she heard about Amber being in one of my lectures. It doesn't even matter. I was so angry the uni had cared about this crap of Lauren's that I got the shits and quit. Completely. So now I have no job and no girlfriend."

Sara put her arms around Jane, but instead of uttering soothing nonsense like her mother had, she ground her teeth right next to Jane's ear and muttered,"...show *her* what for...pfff! Lauren—more like, *Lecturer Lame-arse Fake-Accent!!*"

"Remarkably, Lauren isn't the real bad guy here. The uni's broken. I can't believe how many years I wasted trying to get in good with the dinosaurs that run it. Come on, we'd better get back to your Granny's party." Jane gave her one last squeeze and took them each by the arm as they walked back across the lawn.

"Sorry to cry on you both. I really need to get some friends. My old friends all chose Lauren after the break-up."

Sara made a grossed-out face. "Their loss. They sound like garbage people anyway. Aw, and I love that you cried on me. If you think about it, you've got this exciting blank slate now you quit that shithouse crappy school you were at. I mean, would—I dunno—if you told Amber about it, it could be a sign that you've made some changes?"

Jane sighed. The thought had crossed her mind. She had brought Amber's number up on her phone and had her finger hovering over the call button several times. However, the disappointment in Amber's voice the last time they had spoken rang in her head. She couldn't face letting her down again.

At the end of the day, she knew she wasn't good enough for her. They were too different. Amber needed someone brave, someone strong enough to handle the attention and scrutiny.

"I don't think so, Sare-Bear. Amber and I aren't right for each other."

Sara and Barbara gave each other a loaded look but didn't say anything more.

Sara squeezed her arm as they sat down at the long table.

Even though Jane had had a big cry, she didn't feel any relief. She was weighed down by stones, sinking deeper and deeper into the ocean. She wondered how much further she could sink and still be able to find her way back up to the surface.

Night fell, and her mum blew out the candles on a cake. Jane moved her lips along with the words to "Happy Birthday"—she never sang it because she was worried people would notice how much she butchered the notes.

She stretched her mouth into a smile for family photos, although it felt more like she was doing a grotesque grimace.

The party wore on, and she was thinking she had been there long enough to get away with leaving so she could cry more at home.

Someone plonked down next to her. "What's good, Janey?"

"Hi, Dad."

"How are you, my love?"

"Oh, you know, I've been better."

Her dad didn't know about Amber or the break-up, just that she had quit her job. Her explanation had been that she was "unhappy with the way they handled the recruitment process." Which was the understatement of the century.

He took her hand in both of his. "Sorry it didn't work out for you. That lot can be a bit of an old boys' club. I didn't see it when I was in it, but since I've retired and gained some much-needed perspective, I can see most of them are total wankers."

Jane shouted with laughter. She was shocked out of her sad stupor by her sweet, serious dad, in his bow tie and waistcoat, talking like that.

He laughed along with her. "Even the women! Complete wankers."

Jane wiped a tear (she supposed they were still there, quite ready to be spilled after the last cry).

"There," he patted her hand. "It's good to see you smile."

Jane let her eyes follow the branches of the poinciana, strung with fairy lights. "I've had a couple of calls from other unis. Bigger and even more prestigious. But I don't know." She sighed. "I thought it was all so important. When I was little, I thought you had the best and most distinguished job in the world. Higher education—I took it so seriously."

"I took it seriously too. To a fault at times, I suspect. I'm incredibly lucky to be living this wonderful life. I put it down to dumb luck. The best woman in the world fell in love with me and never figured out that she could do so much better."

Oh no! The tears threatened again. She watched her dad's face as he looked over at where her mum was talking to some friends.

"Ambition, status—none of it means anything without that magic sparkle to make life worth living," he said.

Her mother laughed and twirled around for her friends, showing off the wrap she had draped over her shoulders. It was threaded through with sequins that reflected the party lights. She glittered. The spots of brilliance danced over everyone at the party. It was beautiful.

Jane didn't feel like crying any more. She knew what she needed to do.

CHAPTER 31

"I don't see the harm in just letting her know you're here," said Teddy.

Amber finished the last eleven seconds of a treadmill sprint, then jumped onto the sides of the machine to take a break.

Her trainer, Julio, was in LA, but there was no escaping his strict regimen of workouts, even in a fancy hotel in Brisbane. So an early Friday morning found her in the hotel gym, red-faced and puffed out on the treadmill while Teddy sat in a chair in front of her and scrolled on his phone.

They usually liked to use workout time to go through the day's itinerary and talk through arrangements, but today Teddy was off topic.

"She knows I'm here, all right. I gave her the dates ages ago; we were talking about taking a trip together for a few days."

"Oh." Teddy looked deflated.

Join the club!

Weeks had passed since her last phone call with Jane. It had been a grey blur. Amber had only been able to mark any progression of time by the fact that Teddy looked more and more worried about her every day.

At first, he had been upbeat and employed the tactics he had in his arsenal that had gotten her through her last break-up, mainly loud car singalongs to classic "fuck you" songs, from "I Will Survive" to "You Oughta Know." He had been excited to add a newer track to the rotation: "Single Soon" by Selena Gomez.

In the last few days, however, when it had become clear his tactics weren't working, he had been springing deep and meaningful conversations on her when she least expected it.

"Would you feel better if you had some closure—one last big talk to get it all out in the open?" he had asked one day. "At least you won't die wondering."

Amber was wondering all right, and she was getting deathly sick of it.

She had told Jane not to phone her, and Jane was very black-and-white and followed rules to the letter. Amber had meant it at the time too—she had been angry and hurt, and shocked at Jane's harshness.

The simple fact remained that she had not heard from Jane at all as the weeks had passed. If Jane had wanted to get in contact with her, she would have. Amber hadn't blocked her number. How hard would it have been for Jane to call?

Often Amber imagined how Jane was handling the break-up. She would spin her energy out, picture it hurtling all the way up to Brisbane and looking in on Jane. Sometimes in these daydreams, Jane was just as confused and hurt as Amber was—depressed and driving herself crazy wondering if she had done the right thing.

Sometimes, though, especially late at night, Imaginary Jane had a spring in her step and was relieved to have dodged a high-maintenance relationship with a very needy woman.

The evidence, as it was stacked up and presented to the court, pointed in favour of the latter. Jane had basically called her manipulating and needy on that last day.

And she hadn't phoned.

Amber had convinced herself that if she got in contact with Jane, that second picture of a woman who had moved on with her life would be carved into stone. She didn't think she could bear it.

She missed Jane.

As the days passed, she expected to start getting over it. After all, they hadn't dated that long, and most of it had been long-distance. A kind of despair settled over her when she realised how much she had opened up to Jane, had started to rely on her for emotional support and reassurance.

Maybe Jane had been right—Amber was unhinged and clung on too fast and too hard. Could the connection that she felt have been just in her head?

The rest interval on the treadmill came to an end, and the machine beeped her a countdown. She set off at a slow jog. "You're the one that told me I'm better off, may I remind you?"

He looped his index finger round and round above his head like a lasso. "Roll the tape! I think you'll see you're misrepresenting me. Again."

"For the last time, you're not on a *Selling Sunset* reunion, so stop asking for replays and lie detectors."

He scowled. "Fine. I *may* have suggested—when we were both still very mad at her—that there was still a lot of work to be put into her. The fear of PDA was red-flag adjacent."

Amber's treadmill whirred slightly louder as the pace picked up a notch.

"She didn't like my job," she said, keeping her breathing steady and moving her arms in strong, fluid motions. "It was a minor thing that early in a relationship, but it could have grown to be a massive issue as time went by. I'm sure of it—she never made one concession. Not one. And more than that, anytime there was music, dancing, a heap of people with good vibes, she went stiff as a board. She couldn't get out of there fast enough. It's like she's allergic to joy. I really don't think she's capable of getting past caring what everyone thinks of her. Red flags, Teddy. Big ones."

He stood up and moved next to the treadmill. "OK, sure. But don't you think a part of it may have been shyness? She's been buttoned-up her whole life. And you've always been tuned into the joie de vivre. People your age don't change overnight."

"Watch it."

"Sorry, babes, but it's true. I just think you need to take a really good look at why you're not getting over her. Is there the tiniest shred of doubt, a teensy inkling that you should give her another chance?"

Amber hit the control panel hard with fast jabs, bumping the speed up to a flat-out sprint.

"You can't run away from me!" said Teddy, raising his voice over the whir of the machine.

"Watch me."

"Would you think about giving her a call? I'm worried about how long this low point is going to last."

"She doesn't—care enough about me—to call," Amber gasped between panting breaths. "She definitely doesn't care enough—to change."

Teddy frowned and sat back down.

Amber glanced at him, worried he would keep arguing with her. She was relieved to see him become very interested in something on his phone.

He didn't need to know how much he was testing her last shred of resolve.

She wanted to give in and hear Jane's voice again, but she was scared of the damage Jane could do to her. She had let Jane in more than she had thought possible in such a short time.

Now she was sad and shaken up, but at least she was still in one piece.

CHAPTER 32

Jane tugged on her bow tie, lifting her chin towards her reflection in the mirror inside the lift. *Now it's sticking out!* She huffed and flattened the bow tie back down. She leaned towards her reflection and gave another tug.

"It's fine!" Sara said. "You look great." She stepped forward and adjusted the curl at her own forehead, narrowing her eyes.

"Hey, you two," Teddy said. "This party is full of literal millionaires, interspersed with actual billionaires, maybe. Nobody is going to care what you look like." He pushed between them in the tight space, blocking their view of the mirror while he stared at his reflection and ran his index fingers along his eyebrows.

Jane had texted Teddy that morning, asking for his help. She had been surprised at how easy he was to convince, and anxious to learn that Amber was only in Brisbane for one more night. Now she found herself on the way to a very opulent party in Brisbane's historic City Hall, put on by one of the biggest banks in the country, which claimed to use profits to support music and the arts. Teddy had explained that hosting this annual party and pumping large amounts of money into buying ads on *Australian Idol* were the main ways in which this support was given.

The lift slowed and stopped, making Jane's stomach lurch even more than it already had been all evening. As the doors opened, she was hit with a wall of noise and movement.

"C'mon, c'mon! She's due to arrive in a couple of minutes," Teddy said, beckoning them to follow, then plunging into the crowd of people in suits and floor-length gowns.

Jane kept her eyes fixed on Sara in her hot-pink dress and matching gloves that went all the way up past her elbows. She dodged and weaved between the press of strangers as they talked and laughed loudly.

Finally, they stopped, and Teddy showed three shiny black cards on lanyards to a big man standing next to a velvet rope.

The man nodded and unhooked the rope to let them pass.

The exclusive inner sanctum they were now in was equally noisy from chatter and music being blared by a DJ on a tall platform.

Teddy took Jane and Sara by their arms and steered them so that they were standing in front of him. "OK, I'm going back down to meet her at the car. You two stay out of sight for now."

"Stay out of sight. You mean hide?" Jane yelled over the party noise. All the colours were starting to blur, and the noise was pounding against the inside of her skull.

Teddy either didn't hear her or did a good job of pretending he didn't as he hurried off.

Jane rounded on Sara. "I don't see how we're meant to hide! Stand behind a pot plant? Duck under a table? Sit holding large newspapers with eyeholes cut out?" Her palms were clammy, and her insides had an unpleasant buzz. The plan—which had seemed so sensible when she had talked it out with her accomplices that afternoon—was now an impending disaster. A ham-fisted ambush.

"Do you want to bail? We can leave, and I'll text Teddy." Sara placed her hand lightly on her aunt's arm.

Jane held her gaze and took a breath. *Leave.* She considered it. The relief of being out of the noise and jostling crowd would be tremendous. Plan A had been to phone Amber. She could still do that. It would be the more normal thing to do.

Jane looked up at the ceiling and rolled her shoulders a couple of times. At the best of times, talking on the phone wasn't her strong suit. She never knew what impression she was making. The little visual cues she relied on—a nod, eye contact, a smile—wouldn't be available to her if she phoned Amber. She would mess it all up, just like the last call.

"No, let's stay. This is my last shot. It's too important."

Sara nodded and gave her arm a squeeze. "I think that's a great idea. Hey, can I get you something to drink?"

Jane's mouth was so dry, it was an effort to swallow. "Oh, yes, please. No alcohol. And no sugar either. It will make me jittery."

Sara raised an eyebrow.

Jane scoffed. "OK, you're right. Make me *more* jittery. And no bubbles, please."

Sara patted her hand. "I'm on it."

Jane planted her feet and took some deep breaths.

She couldn't control Amber or her reaction tonight. Amber might not want to talk to her at all, and that would have to be all right. *If I lay it all out with complete honesty, I can walk out of here happy that I did everything I could.* Jane knew she wouldn't be happy if she left the party without Amber, but thinking forward to that possibility made her insides lurch. She tried to gently bring her mind back to the present, as she had been struggling and striving to do all day.

"All righty, one room temperature, plain tap water for you and a Hawaiian margarita for me. Look how many little umbrellas they put in!"

Jane took hold of the glass of water.

Sara looked at her phone. "Teddy says they're back."

Jane's hand started to shake, spilling water over the rim of the glass.

Sara took the glass. "Uh-oh! Wet sleeve alert. They've got serviettes at the bar."

Jane couldn't catch sight of Amber before being whisked away.

"Gah! These heels need to be two centimetres higher. I'm stepping on my front hem."

"The fit is opulent, babes. Totally worth it. Just slide your feet along the floor when you walk, like a bride down the aisle," Teddy replied. He also made a quick adjustment so that the thigh-high split wasn't creeping around the back anymore.

Amber took a few steps and didn't step on her skirt. "Thank you." She took a quick scan of the room and sighed. A few heads started turning her way. Some men in shiny, expensive suits began to make a beeline towards her from across the room.

She needed to stop saying yes to these corporate events. They were an unexpected add-on that came with signing up for her job on network television. The point of her show was to sell advertising spots, and many of *Australian Idol*'s big-name sponsors were represented at this party. Teddy had a list on his phone from the TV network of people Amber was expected to rub shoulders with. She cleared her throat and stood a little straighter, preparing to smile and chat with the shiny-suit guys.

Usually, she would be able to find the fun in a night out on the town, even if the reason for her being there was commercial and empty. But it was hard these days. *Nope! At the very least, tonight can be a distraction from thinking about the break-up.*

"Let's get this over with, Ted," she said through gritted teeth.

"You got it! I've managed to identify all the bigwigs on the list, and they're congregated over there. These guys coming over are complete nobodies. Let's make a move."

"Oh God, yes. Vamoose! Go, go, go," she hissed.

She walked (bride-style, as Teddy had suggested) as fast as her skirt would allow, towards a velvet rope manned by security. Once on the other side, she looked over Teddy's shoulder as he consulted the list on his phone.

"There's Paul Van Der Bakker. Head of advertising for Optimal Telecommunications. They have that ad you like with the cat. He was born in Perth and likes golf."

The grey feeling Amber had been trying to shake settled on her a little more heavily.

Teddy glanced at her, and his eyebrows furrowed. "Hey. Are you OK? We can pull the pin on tonight if you want. It's not like the network's going to fire you. You're giving them *Idol*'s highest ratings since 2008."

"No, no. Let's do it. I didn't sit in hair and make-up for two hours just to turn around and sit in my hotel room all night." She smiled to reassure him. "It's just like a meet and greet. This is what you and I do."

"For sure. Except this meet and greet goes towards your *Idol* wage, which, if we keep this up, might finally allow me to live the life I was born for—flying private instead of commercial."

Amber laughed. "Mate, we could have been flying private all year, but I couldn't deal with the carbon footprint." She laughed again as he put his hands to his face in mock horror.

Teddy grinned. "Let's meet and greet the fuck out of these rich wankers."

"What's she doing now?" Jane stood up and craned her neck.

"Talking to yet another old person. This one's a bald guy."

Her heart pounded as she caught sight of Amber, in profile, at a distance, her mouth curved into a smile at something a man in a suit was saying.

Everything about her shone. Everything—her face and the way she moved—was dear to Jane. It was painful to look at her, and it was painful to not look at her.

Sara pressed down on her shoulder. "Oi, sit. You're too tall, and she's gonna spot you. I've got eyes on Teddy, and I'll tell you when he gives the signal."

Jane sat on the bar stool, one foot and both hands starting to tap wildly. "You better keep your voice down. People are going to think we're part of a kidnap squad."

A woman with a silver helmet of hair raised her eyebrows at Jane before letting her glance slide away.

Jane gnawed on her thumbnail. The woman was right. She was unhinged, and this plan was unhinged. *Let's can it! Pull the plug!*

"That's Teddy's signal! You're on!"

Jane's legs were jelly.

Sara dragged her to her feet.

Amber appeared a little distance in front of her.

The crowd just happened to part, so there was miraculous empty space between them.

Amber looked right at Jane and froze.

Teddy took Amber's hand in both of his.

Jane couldn't hear him, but she had told him what to say—that Jane was here and she wanted to talk to her and that she would just turn around and leave no questions asked if Amber wanted.

Jane held her breath. *He's saying so many words! How is this taking so long?*

He finally stopped talking.

Amber looked at Jane for a long moment. Then she nodded.

She spoke to Teddy again.

He beckoned Jane over, then walked backwards until he was enveloped by the crowd.

Jane willed her feet to move and was shocked when it worked. Her chest thudded. Longing and shame at how she had acted in Melbourne rose in her throat, almost making her feel ready to burst into tears. She balled both her fists. "Hello," she said.

Amber's face was a mask. "You're here. What do you have to say?"

Jane leaned in a little. The room was still so loud. She would have to speak up. The people around wouldn't be able to hear. Or would they? *It doesn't matter! Only one thing matters.* She cleared her throat. "I'm sorry for how I acted. I was unfair to you and cruel. That's not who I am. I'm sorry for all of it. You're so...wonderful and brilliant, and I kept you at arm's length the whole time. Putting my job and my reputation before our relationship. I'm an idiot.

"I've changed. I promise you I've changed. I quit the uni. It was toxic there. But I take full responsibility for what a terrible girlfriend I was. I was paying my past trauma forward to you, which wasn't fair, and I'm so sorry."

Amber's gaze was steady. Her face still showed no emotion. "Do you want me back?"

Electricity jolted through Jane. "Oh, fuck! Did I not say? Yes. Absolutely. Please will you give me another chance? I want to be with you. No conditions, no hiding, proud every day that I'm in your life. Please."

Amber folded her arms slowly. Her throat muscles were tensed, as if fighting strong emotion.

What emotion? Blazing anger? The flush that rose in her cheeks didn't look like forgiveness.

Jane's fingernails pressed painfully into her own palms.

Then Amber inclined her head. "Yep."

Jane's mouth fell open. Furious joy roared in her head. "No! As in, *yep*?"

Amber's eyes shone. "Sure thing. Let's do it."

"Holy shit! Yes? Yes!" Jane took Amber in her arms.

Amber fell against her chest and wrapped her arms around her.

Tears spilled down Jane's cheeks.

Amber looked up at her. "I really didn't know if I was getting an apology, like, as in closure recommended by your therapist, or if you wanted to get back together."

Jane groaned. "Words are not my friend sometimes. But I do have one more question."

"Yeah?"

"Would it be all right if I kissed you?"

Amber smiled and held on tighter to Jane. "More than all right."

Jane leaned in. Her lips touched Amber's, and warmth flowed all the way through her body.

Amber snaked her hand up into Jane's hair and pulled her face down so she could kiss her deeper.

The party disappeared. There was only her and Amber and elation filling her entire body. Amber's lips held tenderness and heat, and Jane gave herself over to both.

After a long moment, Amber pulled away. "Um, yeah. I think we have to get out of here. If I act on what I'm feeling right now, all these people looking at us will be less like 'aw sweet' and more like 'uh, we need to arrest these women for public indecency'."

Jane laughed. "I am right there with you."

"Where's Teddy?"

"He can't be far. Sara was over by the bar."

Amber took Jane's hand.

It was the best feeling Jane could have possibly imagined.

"Oh *I see.* So the whole gang was in on this little scheme. Was it your idea or your crew's to dress you so hot it's making my eyes water?" Amber asked.

Jane scoffed.

"No, really. When I saw you, you really could have snapped your fingers and tossed me a hotel key and I would have followed you."

"No. Really?"

"Ehhhh, who can say for sure? All the apologies and promises were nice too."

Jane lowered her head and spoke seriously. "I meant every word, you know. I'm going to make it up to you. It will be different."

Amber squeezed her hand. "It's already different." She looked up. "Hey, here's the twins from *The Parent Trap,*" she said as Teddy and Sara rushed towards them.

"We were watching," said Sara.

"But not in a creepy way," said Teddy.

"And we didn't want to interrupt," said Sara.

"What's *The Parent Trap?*" asked Teddy.

Jane grinned. "Just an old movie where two Lindsay Lohans have a madcap scheme to get two hopeless middle-aged people back together. Actually, it was Sara's favourite movie growing up."

"And now it's come true!" Sara beamed and squashed Jane and Amber into a massive hug.

"Get in here, Ted," said Amber.

He shrugged and wrapped his arms around the three of them.

As they walked towards the lifts, Amber put her arm around Sara. "It's very nice to see you again, Sara. I love the dress."

"Oh my gosh. You look amazing! I'm so glad you and Jane are back together. Just between you and me, the moping was getting a bit old."

"Bloody hell," said Teddy. "Over here with this one too. Mope, mope, mope. It's like she doesn't know that her smile is what pays my bills."

Amber hung back as Sara pushed the button. She took hold of Jane's arm. "My hotel's right up the street," she whispered.

Desire pulsed through Jane, mingling with the golden glow already there. "Well, geez. Toss me the key and snap your fingers and let's take this reunion to a second location."

"They're kissing again," said Teddy.

"Awwww, look at my gay aunties. Maybe we better let them get this lift by themselves."

"God, yes."

Jane grinned and pulled Amber in after her.

"Teddy, my room key, please!"

"Uh! Yeah, yeah. Here!" He tossed it just as the door closed.

Jane was already kissing Amber again. She felt Amber smile as the key card hit Jane's leg and thwacked onto the floor.

EPILOGUE

One and a bit years later

Jane looked out of her office window and squeezed the bridge of her nose. Surprised to see it was dark outside, she checked her phone for any notifications.

"Worried I wouldn't show?" said Sara, leaning against the doorframe

Jane smiled. "No, I know you can be trusted. Let's get out of here."

After *Australian Idol* wrapped for the year, Jane had moved to LA with Amber and started working for a not-for-profit think tank just south of the downtown area. The organisation aimed to reduce social inequality and discrimination and worked with charities all around the world to put their initiatives into action. She also taught sociology a couple of times a week at a community college in Monterey Park. Many of her students were immigrants or from financially disadvantaged families and were trying to create better lives for themselves.

The work was invigorating. She hadn't realised how weighed down she had been by the university system until she had thrown it off her shoulders. If she ever looked back on the days when she had been with Lauren and the uni politics had been her whole life, she shuddered.

"I checked the traffic," said Sara. "The I-105 looks miraculously clear. We'll be early at this rate."

Jane pulled on her jacket and put her phone in one of the pockets. "I'm glad. But it only takes one bingle for that whole stretch to become slow. Here, give me a hug."

"Aw, bring it in. Would you look at you? You think the thrill of seeing your favourite pop star would have worn off by now."

Jane put her arm around Sara's shoulders as they walked through towards the lifts. "You could have phoned me from the car, you know."

"You know I love coming up here." She looked at the desks at either side and lowered her voice to a whisper. "Your workmates are the coolest people I've ever seen in real life." She greeted a tall woman with a nose ring and tattooed forearms. "Hi, Carmelita."

"Hey Sara. You out of here, Jane?"

"Yes. Amber's home from tour tonight. Flying in from Toronto. We're going to collect her at the airport."

"Tell her hi from me. That new track, "Don't Lecture," is fire."

"Thanks. I will do." She exchanged a glance with Sara. The new song was written from the perspective of someone who wanted to take down a current partner's manipulating ex. The bridge, which included the lyrics *"Don't use the Queen's English to fuck up my baby's business"* had a little dance that people liked to film themselves doing on TikTok. The song was currently number one in Australia and had cracked the Top 20 in the States.

The think tank's offices were in a renovated textiles factory and were not swanky by any means, but Jane loved being there. The energy of her colleagues, some of them younger than her college students, some postretirement but happy to volunteer a few days a week, was infectious. They were passionate about making the world a better place.

Jane drove Sara's car to the airport. She had gotten even more confident with LA traffic in the past year, but freeway driving still made her palms sweat. She did it as often as possible, attempting little by little to conquer her fear.

Sara kept up a pleasant chatter as they drove. She had been thrilled when Jane and Amber had settled in LA, and was often over at their house, helping make dinner or watching TV with them. If she stayed late, there was a guest room that had become her designated space because she slept over so often.

Amber had been away touring on and off throughout the year but had been able to wind it back after she signed a four-year contract to judge on *Australian Idol*. She had told Jane that she hadn't thought she would enjoy it, that TV talent shows were the place washed-up former artists went to die, but that she had unexpectedly fallen in love with it. The excitement and enthusiasm of the budding singers was a constant reminder of why she had chosen her career in the first place.

Jane could do her research work from anywhere, and the *Idol* season lined up well with summer break at the community college, so she was able to spend most of it travelling around Australia with Amber.

She braked as a purple jeep cut in front of her without indicating. Her decrease in speed earned her a honk from the car behind her.

LA seemed massive and out of control compared to Brisbane, but she enjoyed living there. She went to the same gym as Courteney Cox and the same yoga studio as Nicki Minaj (she hadn't known who those people were, but Amber had pointed them out). Jane had started to develop a love of rhythm and expression and so had joined an African drumming circle at a community hall in Eagle Rock on Wednesday nights. Jane missed Amber when she was away, but between work friends, drumming friends, and family, she was never lonely.

Jane parked the car, and she and Sara made it to the arrivals gate in plenty of time.

Sara wandered off to look at the bookstore, and Jane sat watching the gate. She let the anticipation of seeing Amber again and taking her home course around her body. It felt like comfort and happiness. She consciously tried to hold onto and raise up the gratitude that flooded through her. She smiled to herself. *All this hippy-dippy LA stuff has seeped into my brain.*

Amber and Teddy entered the arrivals area through the gate. Amber stood on tiptoes and scanned the seats, starting at the opposite end from where Jane had jumped up out of her seat.

Jane watched Amber look for her. Amber had only been gone less than two weeks on this northern leg of the tour, but seeing her again made affection well up in Jane with such intensity that she pressed both hands to her chest.

Amber's eyes met Jane's, and she broke into a smile of pure joy. She ran over—leaving Teddy with the luggage cart—jumped into Jane's arms, and kissed her.

Jane lifted her up and slowly let her back down, but without breaking the kiss. She would tell her how much she missed her and how glad she was to have her back, but right now she was content with showing her.

Someone cleared their throat, and Jane looked up. Sara and Teddy were standing close by, Teddy looking very impatient to be dropped back at his apartment so he could go to bed.

"Yep, um, sorry, Ted. We'd better go," said Amber.

"Excuse me."

Jane and Amber turned. Two women had been standing off to the side and now approached. They looked to be in their late thirties, and one had an Australian accent.

Amber squeezed Jane's hand as if to apologise for the fan interaction that was about to begin.

Jane squeezed back, to say *no worries*.

"Hi, wow, sorry. We saw you on our flight and couldn't believe it was you! We're huge fans. We're sorry to bother you, but can we get a photo?"

"Of course. Totally. Jump in. It's great to meet you. What are your names?"

Once Amber had charmed them for a little while, Jane put out a hand. "Would you like me to take a photo?" she asked.

"Yes, please, that would be amazing. Hey, wait, aren't you Jane? We see you dancing backstage on Amber's TikTok."

Jane shot Teddy a wry look. He was always the one who posted the candid videos. "Yes, that's me. I'm Amber's partner."

"Oh wow! Hey, will you be in the photo too? You're internet famous!"

Jane was bemused as she handed the phone back over to Sara and stood next to Amber. She was lucky the vast majority of Amber's fans were very nice since she was notorious among them now. Amber didn't let go of Jane's waist after the snaps were taken and goodbyes made. She looked up at her.

Teddy put his head to the side and huffed.

"We'll meet you at the car," said Sara and helped Teddy wheel the luggage away.

"He didn't sleep on the plane, grumpy thing," said Amber.

They set off after them. Amber had both arms slung around Jane's waist, so they made slow progress.

"Those fans were really taken with you," said Amber. "They couldn't give a shit about me after they learned who you were."

"Oh, ha ha. You're their idol, and I'm some weirdo who dances badly. Then Teddy turns it into socials content for cheap likes."

"Well, the Amber Hatfield fandom will be crushed if you and I ever break up."

"Oh, absolutely. If they don't get a regular rotation of my slick dance moves in their feed, there may be riots."

Amber held tighter around Jane's waist.

Jane kissed the top of her head. "Luckily for them, we're not going to break up."

Amber hauled Jane to a stop. "Never ever?" she asked.

"Never ever."

Amber pulled Jane's face down gently and kissed her again.

There was a loud groan of impatience from Teddy up ahead.

"Get a room!" Sara shouted, laughing.

Jane grinned and held Amber tighter.

OTHER BOOKS FROM YLVA PUBLISHING

www.ylva-publishing.com

PERKS OF OFFICE

Liz Rain

ISBN: 978-3-96324-661-6
Length: 178 pages (61,000 words)

Hapless office worker Emma is smacked with an instant crush on Bridget O'Keefe. Her new, untouchable, straight boss. After a political scandal breaks, Bridget turns to Emma for comfort. Is it just a meaningless fling? Because there's no way ambitious, beautiful Bridget wants anything more from Emma. Is there?

A light-hearted, age-gap lesbian office romance.

A QUESTION OF SINCERITY

Sabrina Blaum

ISBN: 978-3-69006-036-3
Length: 287 pages (87,000 words)

Claudia lives by one rule: honesty. When her fun fling turns out to be married to her reserved, buttoned-up new boss, Elizabeth, she's left reeling. But once the truth unravels and the fallout clears, what happens when the two women find they're drawn to each other? Is their attraction a kiss of death or the foundation of something real?

An age-gap, opposites attract lesbian romance where the universe has the last laugh.

SOMETIMES WE FLY

Cheyenne Blue

ISBN: 978-3-69006-015-8
Length: 253 pages (80,000 words)

At forty-six, Maren is Australia's most popular newsreader, but for how much longer? Now her teen daughter is acting out. Something has to change. Jac's new neighbour's kid is causing trouble for her motorcycle business. It'd be so easy to stay mad except that her mum, Maren, turns out to be a gorgeous closeted celeb. That way leads to danger…right?

A closeted celebrity, a furious neighbour, and a whole lot of sexual tension charge this late-in-life, coming-out lesbian romance set in Sydney.

FROM FAN TO FOREVER

Tiana Warner

ISBN: 978-3-96324-691-3
Length: 202 pages (67,000 words)

When student Rachel meets her crush, A-list actress Cate, it leads to a shocking offer to become a science consultant on Cate's new film.

An age-gap lesbian celebrity romance about how much you'd risk to have your dream.

ABOUT LIZ RAIN

Liz is from sunny Queensland, Australia and grew up doing lots of swimming, cricket and netball. She started a degree in journalism but decided early on she didn't want to be a journalist because she heard the hours were long and the pay was bad. She couldn't think of anything else she wanted to study, however, so decided to get the degree anyway.

After that she taught English in Japan, where she joined a soccer team to meet girls. Luckily the captain was a very nice American who is now her wife.

They live quietly in Logan, Queensland with their two daughters and a cat named Carly-Rae. Liz's interests are women's Australian Rules football (especially the Brisbane Lions) and teaching herself the mandolin off YouTube.

CONNECT WITH LIZ

Facebook: www.facebook.com/lizrainwrites

E-Mail: lizrainwrites@gmail.com

The Meet and Greet

Available in paperback and e-book formats.

ISBN (paperback): 978-3-69006-127-8
ISBN (e-book): 978-3-69006-128-5
ISBN (pdf): 978-3-69006-129-2

Published by Ylva Publishing, legal entity of Ylva Verlag, e.Kfr.

Ylva Verlag, e.Kfr.
Owner: Astrid Ohletz
Am Kirschgarten 2
65830 Kriftel
Germany

www.ylva-publishing.com

First edition: 2026

For questions about product safety, please reach out to:
info@ylva-publishing.com

Credits
Edited by Lenir Costa and Michelle Aguilar
Cover Design by Ilona Gostyńska-Rymkiewicz
Print Layout by Ylva Publishing

Image rights cover illustration provided by Shutterstock LLC; iStock; Dreamstime; Canva; AdobeStock; Depositphotos
Graphics provided by Freepik

www.ingramcontent.com/pod-product-compliance
Lightning Source LLC
LaVergne TN
LVHW090942080826
845145LV00003B/853